SWEET TEMPEST

Following in the footsteps of her late father, weather wizard Sherman Tucker, Florida meteorologist Kelly Tucker loves the exhilaration of flying through gales to reach the eye of a hurricane. And just as thrilling is her chance meeting with daredevil storm chaser Ross King. During the heat of a tropical tempest Kelly becomes attracted to Ross — despite believing him to be responsible for her father's death in a violent tornado. When someone tries to sabotage her work and destroy her father's legacy, Kelly turns to Ross for help. Suddenly she finds herself hurled into a whirlwind of danger, betrayal and turbulent desire . . .

Books by Patricia Werner
Published by The House of Ulverscroft:

THE WILL
PRAIRIE FIRE
IF TRUTH BE KNOWN
JENNY'S STAR

PATRICIA WERNER

SWEET TEMPEST

Complete and Unabridged

ULVERSCROFT
Leicester

First published in the United States of America
in 1999

First Large Print Edition
published 2008

The moral right of the author has been asserted

British Library CIP Data

Werner, Patricia
    Sweet tempest.—Large print ed.—
    Ulverscroft large print series: romance
    1. Love stories
    2. Large type books
    I. Title
    813.5′4 [F]

    ISBN 978–1–84782–406–6

Published by
F. A. Thorpe (Publishing)
Anstey, Leicestershire

Set by Words & Graphics Ltd.
Anstey, Leicestershire
Printed and bound in Great Britain by
T. J. International Ltd., Padstow, Cornwall

This book is printed on acid-free paper

Acknowledgements

Thanks to Rick Hansen for delving into his aeronautics past and answering questions about flying. Thanks to Tracy Bernstein, editor par excellence, without whom this never would have happened. And thanks to my husband, James Werner, who puts up with being married to a writer.

Prologue

Windman, they had called him that night after the junior high school science fair. His experiment making warm water evaporate over a pan of salt water had been nothing unusual. But the heated air had risen in his little glass aquarium to fog the glass. A fan at the top drew the air upward. The glass was cooled by ice, making the air condense and form rain droplets that returned to the pan.

A second fan blew air into holes cut into the side of the aquarium to produce a swirl of air. He couldn't reproduce the earth's rotation, but it didn't matter. He had made a small tornado.

They dubbed him Windman and it had stuck. And years after that simple childhood experiment, he was still fascinated by the same questions pondered by others concerned about the weather. Why do hurricanes form? Why do some get stronger and others fizzle? Why do they follow such erratic paths? He couldn't help the thrill of elation at the last question.

To help release some of his nervous energy, he went to the glass hutch and got down a

1

large brandy snifter. Then he uncorked the new bottle of his favorite cognac and turned up the volume of Vivaldi's *Four Seasons* playing on his stereo. He looked out his picture window at the curtain of rain pounding down.

Pinpoints of light were barely visible in the distance, a wobbly row of them that he knew came from an exceedingly bland government building at the Air Force base. Someone was still at work.

'Fools,' he muttered. Then he lifted his glass in salute to the offshore tropical depression that was causing the rain.

Soon the weather would make him a very wealthy man.

1

Kelly Tucker began her second day at the Gulf Coast Hurricane Center thinking about Ross King. She really shouldn't have been so surprised to see him last night. Still the sight of the tall, dark-haired, devil-may-care computer modeler had caused her a stab of resentment.

What did the team need a reckless stormchaser like King for? Her late father's assistant had always rubbed her the wrong way. And she just wasn't prepared to reopen the old wound of her father's death. But it would be hard not to with Ross on the same team. However, she would try to avoid a confrontation. She needed this job, and she couldn't afford to light the fuse of old resentments that would endanger her concentration for the work at hand.

Kelly pushed her long, straight, medium blond hair back over her ear and folded her tall, equally straight body to sit in the chair in front of her computer, glancing unobtrusively right and left. Her cause for wariness had been waiting for her yesterday in this very same swivel chair. A folded, white piece of paper with block print letters.

GO BACK TO BOULDER.
YOU'RE NOT WANTED HERE.

It had been written with a common felt-tip pen, such as any of the team members might possess.

A nasty feeling of apprehension crawled through her stomach again as she thought about it. She had told no one, but had slipped it into her gray metal drawer. Now she peeked in to see that it was where she'd left it yesterday.

If the sight of her old rival, Ross King, had caused her aggravation, it was probably because the day had started out so badly. Whoever had written the note would probably want her to appear upset and complain to the director. But she had acted as if nothing had happened. It would frustrate the sender to think that perhaps she hadn't even read the note. Or if she had, that she could laugh it off as unimportant.

The director already had enough problems. When he'd greeted her yesterday, he had admitted that he'd been coming down hard on everybody. Some corrupted computer files had caused errors in their weather predictions, something that was intolerable at the Hurricane Center.

Having assured herself that no more

4

threatening notes had appeared overnight, Kelly walked past the other computer workstations arranged in a large horseshoe, and headed for the briefing room. This was a large room with white, aluminum-framed, dry-erase boards spanning the front. A rolled chart was pulled down for today's briefing. Long tables formed three rows, where the flight crew would sit. A certain grayness permeated the room, in spite of the overhead lights Kelly flipped on as she entered.

She peered out the second-floor windows of the plain government building at MacDill Air Force Base. It was a dreary morning in Tampa, Florida. The hard-driving rain made it harder to see the four-engine turboprop that would soon be taking Kelly and a team of weather scientists up to the storm. And into it.

Her adrenaline bumped up a notch at the thought, in spite of all the months of preparation. Standing by the window, she could feel the static electricity making her hair stick to her jumpsuit, and her spine tingled.

'Doesn't look so reassuring, does it?' said a deep, reverberating voice.

She was startled out of her reverie by the last person she wanted to see: Ross King, all densely packed six feet of him.

He was just zipping his blue jumpsuit over an oyster white cotton shirt and khaki trousers, and smiling that perfect, gleaming smile she'd spotted from across the room last night.

She shivered a little at the tumult of wind, rain, and engine noise outside. And at all the unspoken feelings accumulated since she'd last seen him, at her father's funeral six years ago.

'Which doesn't look reassuring, the weather or the P-3?' she asked in her morning husky voice as he came to stand next to her.

The flying laboratory in which they were about to embark was no ordinary airplane. The WP-3 Orion carried radar on its belly and the huge cone on the tail. A boom-mounted gust sensor was located in the probe that stuck out of the utilitarian, gray nose. The name *Hercules* was painted on the fuselage.

The yellow-suited maintenance crew were going over the aircraft, making final preparations. But she was distracted by Ross's presence.

Six years had gone by, but there were the same warm mahogany eyes that seemed to miss nothing. His serious mouth was closed over those straight, even teeth now. The angles of his face were still devilishly handsome, ready to charm the socks off innocent bystanders. And the same inner unconquerable fire was there in the golden flecks in his eyes. His charisma shook her and angered her at once. She would need to keep her distance — for several reasons.

'I guess I was referring to the weather,' Ross said quietly, looking out the window again. 'That's what we came for. They tell me our second home out there is the most reliable weather reconnaissance plane the base has ever had.'

He brought his glimmering eyes back to hers, causing an unsettling feeling in her stomach. 'Hank Jessup's a veteran pilot.'

'True.'

In fact, Hank was one of the most experienced pilots ever to fly into a hurricane to gather research data. The rest of the team's credentials were stellar as well. Hurricane hunters, they were called. And now she was one. Pride and fright mingled. Daddy would have been proud of her.

Ross leaned on the edge of the window frame, appearing to watch the ground crew move around the plane. His brown hair was thick and soft-looking, short-clipped but styled so that just the right amount fell across his forehead. There was no denying the sex appeal that his snug jumpsuit enhanced. He looked more mature and filled out than when he'd been a graduate student six years ago. But she'd bet the years hadn't mellowed any of his showy risk-taking. Always had to be the hero. Well, he wasn't a hero the day her dad had gotten killed.

With effort, she brought her thoughts back to their present conversation.

'I was born in tornado alley,' she said, as they watched the rain. 'And I've studied eighty-mile-an-hour winds in Boulder. But hurricanes are so . . . ' She hesitated, looking for the right word. 'Vast.'

He nodded, his lips relaxing as he continued to watch the flight crew out the window. 'I know what you mean. You're never ready for it.'

Like hers, his voice had just a touch of Southern softness to it. And his words had a rhythm that matched the hint of a drawl in her own voice, in spite of the years away from Oklahoma. She knitted her brows, trying to concentrate on business again.

Kelly was from a small town just outside of Tulsa, and a family who was always close to the land. They were simple, good people whose lives depended on the weather, and she had grown up wanting to give farmers the information they needed to grow successful

8

crops, and to provide warnings that would save lives. It was why she was willing to take the risks that sometimes accompanied the job, even though it scared her sometimes.

And it was why Kelly had left home and come here to Tampa on loan from the National Center for Atmospheric Research in Boulder, Colorado. There was so much to learn. And they'd told her this would be a real feather in her cap. After this, prospective employers would fight for her.

'I've been a visiting scientist at other weather stations,' she said slowly. 'But this is the first time I've ever flown into a storm.'

She was hesitant to admit any wariness to Ross.

'Your dad would be proud of us both, I think,' said Ross. His voice was steady, unafraid to talk about the thing that lay between them. Testing the waters.

The sharp reminder twisted inside her. But one of them had to bring it up. He looked at her then, a look of deep concern in his face.

'How have you really been doing, Kelly?'

'Fine.'

It was an automatic response, with chin uplifted. She knew what he was asking, and she wasn't as ready as he was to talk about it. How was she doing since her father had left Annie and her alone? Had she forgiven Ross for not preventing her father's accident? Had she forgiven herself for not being there that day?

She and Ross and her father had shared a common ground. Now she and Ross were carrying on the work of learning what made weather happen. His computer simulations would help the scientists at the Hurricane Center figure out where hurricanes were going and how strong they were going to get. But there was too much between them. If she'd known he was going to be on this team, she probably wouldn't have come.

The hum of conversation announced more of the jumpsuited meteorologists and flight crew coming into the briefing room. They talked in groups, some leaning and some sitting on the edge of the table. Then the director of the Gulf Coast Hurricane Center strode in.

'Listen up,' said Wilson Quindry.

He was a beefy man of medium height, with wire-rimmed glasses and slightly heavy jowls. He was wearing a short-sleeved shirt and khaki pants.

He wasted no time, but picked up a rubber-nosed pointer and tapped on the unrolled chart depicting the southeast coastline of the United States, the Gulf of Mexico, and the Atlantic basin. He flipped a wall switch, and the chart was softly lighted from above.

'Tropical Storm Isaac turned into a hurricane at oh-six-hundred, one hour ago,' he said.

Kelly moved to the side of the gathering to be able to better see around the burly shoulders of some of the male members of the team. She was hardly small at five-feet-nine, but a good number of the flight crew and researchers gathered there were tall and broad-shouldered. She already wondered if one of them might have left her the unwelcome note. But why? It didn't make sense. She hadn't ruffled any feathers that she knew about. As her gaze passed over the men's faces, her chest tightened. There was hatred in that note. But no time to think of the reasons now.

Ross positioned himself on her right, folding his arms in front of him, legs in a wide stance. She couldn't deny the male heat about him, the kind that most women would want to soak up. But she wasn't one of them. Not back then, not now, not ever.

At the same time, she sensed the mounting tension in the room. The moment had come to fly into the center of an actual storm. Like an oak leaf in a rainstorm, she'd once heard it said.

When Wilson had welcomed her yesterday,

11

he had assured her that the flights into the storm would be as safe as they could make them. But he was more concerned about not getting any more erroneous data transmitted back to base.

Wilson continued his briefing. 'Based on Doppler readings and the satellite scans you've all seen, Hurricane Isaac's headed north by northeast at ten degrees. That could mean landfall in nine hours. We've got to work fast on this one.'

Wilson had been a personal friend of Kelly's dad for years, and she knew that behind his gruff voice was the genuine concern for his colleagues and for the work.

He tapped the chart. 'You will meet up with the storm in less than two hours and enter from the southwest quadrant. Your data will be critical to the coastal warnings.'

Kelly knew how Wilson sweated over the data that came in from these missions. It was up to him to decide whether or not to recommend evacuation of specified coastal areas in the path of the storm. So the Hurricane Center's predictions had to be as accurate as possible. Wilson kept a list of people who'd died from hurricanes to remind him that they were talking about human lives. The gravity of their work was no small thing.

She and Ross happened to exchange

glances, and the tingle she felt between her shoulder blades told her he was thinking the same thing. But she was certain that their unfortunate shared past was going to be a barrier, not a bond. Why then, was she noticing how self-confident, serious, and attractive he looked in that flight suit?

Wilson faced them sternly, the blue eyes behind the wire-rimmed glasses looking at each of the team members in turn.

'I don't need to tell you what a vital role each of you plays. We have to know what's happening with these storms while they are well out to sea. Do your jobs well, and lives will be spared.'

He began to give final assignments.

When he got to Kelly, he relaxed his face into proud appraisal. 'As you all know, Kelly Tucker will be along for the ride this time. If this young lady is anything like her old man, she knows her stuff.'

Kelly gave a self-conscious smile and a tiny shrug of her slim shoulders.

'Thanks,' she said, uncomfortably aware of everyone looking at her. 'Glad to be here.'

It was true that she was proud to be Sherman Tucker's daughter. He had made a name for himself at the University of Oklahoma chasing tornadoes across the plains to gather important data. Everyone in this room knew of his work. And that his passion had killed him.

Hank Jessup came toward her. The pilot was a solidly built man of Ross's height, about ten years older than Ross's thirty. Hank's thick, dark blond hair combed back from a high forehead and creases at the corners of his hazel eyes and around his mouth only distinguished his mature appearance. He and Ross clasped hands solidly. Hank winked at Kelly and spoke in a lazy drawl.

'They say we're all crazy, you know. Flying in rough weather is my business, but people like you two, doing your jobs on this kind of ride — well, I guess you must have your own reasons.'

'Guess we do,' said Kelly. She tried to make it light, though they all knew there was more meaning here than any of them said. 'Mother Nature seems to be our last frontier.'

'Every storm's different,' Hank warned. 'We never know what we'll find when we get there. Here's to a good mission. You let us know if there's anything you need up there.'

Pilot, copilot, and the rest of the flight crew went ahead into the corridor, and then Ross fell in beside Kelly in a firm stride. At the glass door leading outside, they put on ponchos to protect themselves from rain

14

beating down on the tarmac and waited until the flight crew disappeared from the gangway into the interior of the plane. The other two observing meteorologists were still behind them in the briefing room with Wilson, so she found herself alone with Ross again. Her nerves tingled, and he wasn't helping any.

He hovered beside her, his hand on the door ready to open it. 'Scared?'

An edge of excitement chased through her in spite of her apprehension. She looked at the glass, seeing a shadowy reflection of her face there. It was time to put that feather in her cap.

'I've waited for this for a long time,' she admitted. 'But I'd be a fool not to realize the danger.' And then there was the note, but she wasn't going to mention that, especially not to him.

She cocked her head, straightened it again, and studied him. 'How about you? Do you ever get scared?'

He shrugged. 'Sure.'

His glance rested on her face a moment longer than she felt was comfortable. She knew what he was thinking. That she was her father's daughter.

'Ready to go?' he asked gently.

She nodded. He moved his arm, the door opened, and then they were both dashing through the wet. He let her go first as they clanged up the metal steps of the boarding ramp, and then they were inside the hatch of the protective body of the airplane.

Once their ponchos were removed and stowed, they moved aside for the two other members of the observation team to rattle up the metal steps behind them.

There were no seats in the rear of the cabin, which was crammed with research instruments. Three radar systems and four computers rested on coiled steel shock absorbers. Crew members were tightening the heavy straps that held everything in place as Kelly and Ross squeezed around the metal boxes and avoided tripping on coiled-up cords.

Their workstations were on the right side of the plane just behind the wing. Lightning flashed in the overcast, punctuating Kelly's thoughts. She was finally living a dangerous dream. Her father had chased tornadoes on the ground. She was flying into storms in the sky.

Across the aisle from them sat the weather navigator. Garrulous, dark-haired Enrico DeMarcos smiled and bowed from his tight spot.

'Welcome to our humble abode in the sky. I hope she treats you well today,' he said in his Italian accent.

'Thank you, Enrico,' Kelly replied, a tentative smile on her face.

His Latin smile made her feel as if they were embarking on a serenaded gondola ride on a canal in Venice rather than on a scientific aerial data-gathering venture. She studied him briefly. Surely someone with his sunny charm would not harbor the kind of hatred that would cause a person to write a threatening note.

Ross bent across her to peer out the window. When he eased back into his seat, his expression changed into a more pensive one. She looked out the window at the looming mass of clouds ahead. She knew he must be thinking about storm chasing with her dad. She made an effort to ease the awkwardness of being thrown together like this.

'Different, isn't it?'

He gave an ironic grimace. 'Yes. Ten thousand feet in altitude different.'

They were joined by meteorologist Max Omari, who gave them a solemn nod as he took his seat forward of Enrico on the left side of the aisle and busied himself at his workstation. Omari was a German immigrant and an early colleague of Kelly's father as well. She was anxious to talk to him about the work the two of them had done as pioneer storm chasers on the plains of Oklahoma ten years ago. Could he have written yesterday's note? If so, why? She hadn't seen him in more than six years.

Enrico DeMarcos interrupted them. 'GPS check,' he said. He passed Kelly a small black case.

'Thanks.'

She took the case from him and opened it. The global positioning system would provide more precise three-dimensional positioning of the storm and more accuracy at higher altitudes. She'd just learned to use it, poring over the instructions for two days.

'You should have no trouble. When I tell you to pinpoint the position of the storm, we'll check it with the on-board navigational system. Okay?' His dark eyes flashed, accepting her as an equal.

'No problem.'

She and Ross busied themselves with equipment checks and finally leaned back in their seats. She tried to avoid glances to the side, for when she did, she couldn't help noticing Ross's firm chin, pronounced cheek-bones, and set, full mouth. He exuded a sexy confidence that had always unnerved her. Everything about him seemed to speak of advantages and success. He'd always had a way about him that had gotten him what he wanted. She assumed it still did.

She shut the black instrument box and fastened her seat harness for takeoff. There would be nothing to see but drizzle out the side windows for a while. Her thoughts returned to the threatening note she'd found on her chair yesterday, and she tried to ponder the other team members. Unfortunately, that was hard with Ross King sitting beside her. She couldn't help a sizzling awareness of his presence. She reminded herself that she hated sexy, charming men. And this one in particular had never answered for his part in the day her father had been killed.

Ross gave her a thumbs-up as the plane got under way. They didn't speak again until they were airborne.

★ ★ ★

As they bumped along in the overcast, Ross studied the details of the crowded cabin and its occupants. The wind was on the port quarter, and they flew as high as they could to avoid turbulence.

'All right, folks,' Hank's voice came over the intercom. 'Okay to unfasten harnesses.'

Ross and Kelly unhooked the clasps that held the straps across their shoulders and torsos and let their metal clasps clang to the side. They would need the harnesses later when they entered the storm, but they would have an hour or so to move about the cabin before then.

'Guess I'll take some readings.' Ross sat forward and scrutinized the gauges and dials.

The wind-torn clouds cleared a little and he glanced past Kelly out the window again. They were flying over Sanibel Island, where some of the damage from Hurricane Gordon in '94 was still visible from up here.

Beside him, Kelly shook her head, her shiny, strawcolored hair gathered in a band and tucked into the back of her jumpsuit. The static made some of it float upward like soft angel hair. He had the instinctive urge to touch it, but kept his hand still.

He'd read all the resentment and the flash of pain in her eyes when she'd first seen him. She couldn't know that he shared her pain. That he'd never forget the day she'd lost her father. He'd tried to tell Sherman they were too close to that tornado. But he couldn't change his mentor's mind. Any more than he could change the way Kelly felt about him. Or the fact that they'd had to fight over her dad's attention in the first place. He sure missed the old man. But he had to concentrate on the present. It was hard to be with Kelly again. He wanted to reach out and touch her, to comfort each other, but he knew she didn't want that. She was too independent to want anything like that. As far as she was concerned, Ross was part of that horrible day. And it hurt her to see him again.

She furrowed her brows as she looked out the window in deep concentration. 'All the destruction is terrible,' she commented.

Ross nodded solemnly. 'Yes, it is. Better predictions, more lives saved.'

As a fighter pilot, he'd seen too much death. Following the Gulf War, Ross had decided to use his skills in situations that would help prevent disasters. He'd enrolled in graduate school at the University of Oklahoma and gained the computer skills to become a storm modeler.

He pondered the other crew members, thinking about the separate paths that had led them all there, including Kelly's path. Why had she accepted this assignment?

They passed the island and then Kelly made some calculations at her workstation as the turboprop chewed through the winds. She must have sensed him watching her and looked up at him. Then they both looked away. She still had the same classic beauty. Dark blond brows; long, slender nose; and full, sexy mouth. And her voice still had that soft twang and a little natural huskiness to it.

She was more filled out, but still lithe and athletic. He smiled at her while she wasn't looking, and then glanced away. He didn't want her to think he was comparing her to the way she'd looked six years ago. But he was, and she looked good.

'Ever been on hurricane mission before?' she asked.

She studied him with those deep green eyes fringed with dark blond lashes.

'No, this is the first.'

He retreated for a moment into his past. 'But it's the same sort of tension you feel just before a combat mission.'

'Like your missions in the Gulf.'

She seemed to say it without any resentment. She used to criticize his boldness. Hot dog, she'd called him. Well, he didn't take unnecessary risks anymore. Only calculated ones.

She gave him a sidelong glance. 'So what have you been doing since you left OU?'

'After I got my graduate degree, I came back east. I've just been working, doing computer models of storms.'

She didn't seem to notice his vagueness; she nodded, staring out the window. 'Still trying to answer all the questions . . . '

He wasn't sure he was expected to answer.

It was getting darker outside, and the layers

of clouds were denser. He could see the wing tips, but not much else. Then they felt a bigger bump of turbulence and grabbed for their seat harnesses at the same instant the harness light turned on.

'Okay, folks,' Hank's voice came over the intercom. 'Time to check your equipment. Make sure everything's strapped down.' The pilot snapped off the intercom.

The sky had darkened. The sea below was a dark, choppy green with forty-foot whitecaps smashing into each other.

'I don't think we want to ditch the plane today,' said Enrico from across the aisle.

They had drilled the ditching procedure, but who were they kidding? Ross thought. They all knew there would be little chance for survival in an ocean being torn apart by winds of 90 to 150 miles per hour.

They fastened themselves in with the harnesses that crossed the chest from both sides as well as the strap across the waist. They could still reach the built-in work counter stretched across their laps and Ross tried to concentrate on his readings in spite of the bumpy turbulence. Kelly was writing rapidly, jotting down wind speed, humidity, temperature, and air pressure. He saw the grim determination on her high cheekbones, straight mouth, and firm, angular chin as she struggled to take notes in the bouncing plane.

A few moments later, thicker clouds started to envelop the plane, and they could see nothing more as they were folded within the fringes of the storm. Lightning flashed all around as howling wind joined the roar of the engines, and suddenly the plane dropped from under them.

Then a powerful updraft punched the bottom of the plane. Without thinking, Ross brought his hand down over Kelly's and gripped it tightly. Three seconds later, a severe downdraft plummeted the plane toward the churning ocean.

Kelly didn't speak, but her face lost its color.

The left wing dropped, and Ross's stomach felt like it was in his throat. They would have been thrown around in the plane like billiard balls but for their seat harnesses. This was rough, even for experienced flyers.

A second later, power surged in the engines, and Hank had the plane's nose up again. Murmurs of relief swept through the cabin. Ross relaxed his grip on Kelly's hand and sent her a look just to reassure himself that she was all right. He glanced at the gauge in front of him, which had calculated the downdraft at a gut-wrenching 1,200 feet. His internal calculator agreed.

Suddenly Kelly was fumbling with her harness and Ross was shocked to see the shoulder straps come loose in her hands. With round, frightened eyes, she stared at the ends of the straps that should have been secured to the seat behind her head. He could see the tear where only a few strands had held her in. The jolt of the plane had torn the remaining threads.

A spurt of anger surged through his gut. How could broken strap fastenings not have been spotted by the ground crew going over the plane? When the plane yawed again, she could be seriously hurt.

'Hang on to me,' he commanded. The turbulence wasn't over yet.

2

Ross planted his right arm across her chest and gripped the metal frame of the workstation, pressing her against the back of her seat. She did as he said and grasped the arm he had pressed against her. Her lips tightened just before an updraft hurled them skyward and her fingers dug into his sleeve to hang on. They were at the eye wall, where columns of wind soared upward at more than thirty miles per hour.

She felt three times the pull of gravity, as her whole body pressed into the seat. The plane pitched and yawed, shaking so violently, she was sure that death was near. Fear lodged in her throat as she hung on to Ross's muscular arm. *This is normal*, she tried to remind herself. *Hank knows what he's doing.*

But she wasn't harnessed in.

It'll be over in a minute, she tried to telegraph to herself, praying for safety.

Then they broke out of the overcast and entered brighter clouds. A shaft of sunlight probed the clouds and then bright sunlight flooded the cabin, making her blink. The plane stopped its gyrations. Out the window, she could see high walls of white cumulus all around the circular clear area in the center.

The intercom crackled and Hank's voice announced, 'We're in the eye.'

The plane's course was smooth now, but Kelly was shaking from head to toe.

'You okay?' asked Ross.

She tried to nod and make a sound that indicated yes. A little sheepishly she pried her fingers loose from his arm, and he eased it away from her slowly. But his hand stopped to give her cold ones a warm squeeze that helped flow life back into her.

'We'll talk to Wilson about that harness as soon as we get back,' he said angrily. 'That should never have happened.'

Her heart turned over in her chest, both from fright and in gratitude for his concern. She was incredibly aware of his masculine nearness as he hovered over her protectively. It was almost as if he really cared about her. Her lips felt clamped together. After making sure she was still breathing, she spoke in a low voice.

'I'm all right now,' she said, trying to arrange her expression into one that would reassure him. 'Better not make a fuss about it 'til we get back to base.'

His liquid brown eyes seemed to hold a trace of doubt, and she felt her heart start to hammer for a different reason. His strong, confident demeanor in the face of danger made her shake with the desire to be held. Surely this was just an overreaction to the sudden scare.

Stop it, she tried to tell herself.

'Broken equipment happens sometimes,' she said, trying to make light of it, even if she didn't feel that way. 'I'd rather not draw attention to it right now.'

'If you're sure.'

He still leaned toward her, a frown on his face as if her safety were far more important than the fact that they were now flying inside a hurricane.

'I'm sure,' she said.

Self-consciously she slipped her hand out of Ross's grip and leaned toward the window to peer out, letting her heart settle down. The eye wall towered above them as far as she could see, cyclonic winds howling all around the tranquil vortex. She felt her lips part as she gazed at the sight. The scare was over now. This was what they had come for.

'Look at that,' she said, squinting upward. Far above them, she saw blue sky. This was even more amazing than she had expected. A new poignant thought slipped through her tangled emotions.

'Dad would have loved this,' she couldn't

help saying out loud.

'Agreed,' replied Ross, who leaned over to look out the window. 'But look down there.'

Far below, the gnashing sea was still a green writhing beast with tops of big waves torn off and carried away in a white, boiling sheet.

To her embarrassment, Kelly felt tears threaten, whether in a delayed reaction to the fright over the broken harness or in awe at the incredible experience. She took a moment to get control of herself.

Scientists and crew got up to move around in the stand-up cabin and compare notes. Ross patted her hands.

'While we're in the eye, the ride will be smooth. We can take a stretch and look around. It's okay to get up.'

Now that her scare was over, Kelly was almost amused by his silky, soothing tone. Any other woman would have been swept off her feet by the concern his deep glances were communicating, except that she doubted her feet would hold her just now. And she wasn't any other woman.

'Hank won't turn on the fasten seat belt light until he really means it,' Ross said, humor lightening the mood.

She returned his smile with stiffer lips than his own. 'I think I'll keep my seat for now.'

He got up and left her, moving forward to talk to the pilots.

Left alone, she gathered her thoughts for work, preparing to take the readings from the global positioning system. It should give her their exact altitude, latitude, and longitude, taken from two points on the horizon below and one point from a satellite traveling around the earth's equator.

She steadied her hands to lift the piece of equipment out of its case and set it on the work counter in front of the monitors. Then she turned the knob to 'on,' just as she was supposed to.

But instead of the red light and silent movement of needles across the dials, the black box let out a screech that assaulted her ears. Conferring in the aisle beside her, Max and Enrico both turned and stared.

'What are you doing?' asked Enrico, raising his hands to cover his ears.

She shook her head, and switched it off. 'Sorry, I don't know. I just turned it on and it screeched.'

She fiddled with the other settings, knowing full well that what was making it scream might not be evident from the outside. But she had to try it again.

She glanced up at Enrico and Max, who were watching her carefully. Max frowned at the instrument in his scholarly way, his wire-rimmed glasses circling small gray eyes in a middle-aged, creased face.

'Here goes one more time.'

She turned the knob, and again the harsh sound filled the cabin.

'Enough,' yelled Enrico, holding his hands over his ears until she turned it off.

Clearly she couldn't take any readings with the offensive sound. The GPS would have to wait. A spiral of frustration coiled within her. First the note, then the broken straps, now this. Her first mission was turning into a fiasco!

Ross made his way back, and the other scientists made room for him until his suited torso filled the aisle beside his seat.

'You should go up and see the view from the nose,' he said with a smile. 'It's pretty spectacular.'

His eyes glimmered down at her, and her heart lurched at the special concern he was showing her. It was just because of their shared relationship with her father, of course. That was all. When she had a chance to talk to him privately, she'd have to make it clear that he didn't need to do that.

Still distracted by the GPS malfunction and the aftermath of the bumpy ride with no harness, she gazed uncertainly forward.

'How long will we be in the eye?'

'Long enough for you to take a look. I'll stay here.'

'This thing doesn't seem to work.' There was irritation in her voice, and she frowned at the black box with its needles and dials. 'It squeals when you turn it on.'

'So I heard.'

She caught his grimace as he glanced around the cabin as if looking for someone to accuse.

He waited until she struggled out of the seat. Quarters were so close that she had to flatten herself against him to get past him in the aisle. She turned her head to avoid an embarrassing acknowledgment of the enforced proximity. But she felt his warmth. His touch on her elbow was meant for assistance, but an unmistakable tingle sprang through her as she grasped an overhead loop to help steady herself.

Then she slid past and worked her way to the cockpit, where the solid glass windows offered a breathtaking 180-degree view. Hank and the copilot were wedged in between their instruments with straps across their chests and waists. Headsets connected them to the radio. Tiny red lights blinked on the wide console with everything in arm's reach. There was just room for her to sit on a padded jump seat between them.

'Hi, Kelly,' Gray Worther, the copilot, shouted above the roar of the aircraft.

'Hello, Gray.'

He was a wiry man with a balding pate and choppy features. A friendly grin revealed smoke-stained teeth.

She sucked in her breath at the sight inside the eye of the storm. It was a place of incredible serenity and beauty, perfectly shaped, puffy and white. Tall, bulging cumulus sloped upward to thirty thousand feet or so.

'Pretty awesome, huh?' said Gray in the loud voice they had to use in the cockpit.

'Sure is,' she shouted back.

Then she noticed flocks of birds circling inside the eye. She pointed. 'Where have those birds come from?'

'A lot of storms carry birds with them,' Gray replied. 'They must get blown in and have enough sense not to try to fly out. Birds from Florida sometimes end up as far from home as New Jersey.'

She shook her head and smiled at the image of the poor birds being transplanted.

She stayed forward for a quarter of an hour, the pilots answering her questions. Finally, Hank asked her to take her seat.

'We'll be penetrating the west wall as soon

as Ross and Max drop the navigation receiver,' he said, referring to the instrument that would sail to earth on a parachute and send signals back to the plane. 'Might get a little bouncy.'

Vast understatement, Kelly thought. A little dagger of emotion pierced her heart. Danger or no, this was what she'd come for. How many people got to fly into the eye of a storm? She felt the goose bumps rise.

Here I am, Daddy, she said to herself, closing her eyes briefly. She had the feeling he knew she was up here.

Before she left the cockpit, she thought of mentioning the broken harness, but hesitated. Now wasn't the time. They would tell Hank and Wilson when they got back to base. Then they would have time to do something about it.

★ ★ ★

Ross accompanied Max Omari to the rear of the packed aircraft to drop the instrument that would transmit the storm's temperature profile, wind speed, direction, and other data back to the plane. A man of middle height in his fifties, Max moved along carefully. Their steps rattled on the metal floor of the equipment bay, and Ross was glad for their flight suits. The temperature in the plane was uneven, and it was cold in the rear.

After the apparatus was dropped, Enrico would receive the data at his listening post and then pass it to Johann Amundsen, the weather officer. Johann would relay that information to the Hurricane Center for forecasting.

Hank's voice came over the intercom box fixed to the bulkhead. 'Okay, gentlemen, let her go.'

Ross flipped a switch on the intercom to reply. 'Roger that.'

He assisted Max as he inserted the instrument into a tube, then slid the tube into a vacuum compartment and shut the lid. Max turned the crank that sealed the compartment, then nodded at Ross. *Man of few words*, thought Ross.

Max indicated a switch on a control panel and nodded again. Ross flicked the switch while Max pressed a lever beside the vacuum tube. They heard a thump as the tube was released from the belly of the plane. In a few minutes, when the plane banked, they could see the bright red and orange parachute open to ease the instrument's trip to the ocean.

'How long will it take her to reach the ocean?' Ross asked, peering out the window.

'Perhaps thirty minutes,' said Max. 'It will

depend on the conditions.'

He had the precise enunciation of someone who spoke English as a second language. Ross knew from the background reports he'd read that Max had come to America with his parents after World War II.

'Of course.' Ross smiled in acknowledgment.

Their task taken care of, Max brushed his hands together, indicating that they were finished here. They worked their way up the aisle again.

For another forty-five minutes, everyone took readings and compared observations. The storm pinpointed, they were finally ready to fly out of the eye. Ross insisted on trading seats with Kelly. He wanted to make sure she was strapped down securely, while he'd take his chances holding on.

'But . . . ' She tried to make an argument, but evidently could think of none.

Finally she demurred and got up so that he could slide in first. At least the waist strap on the window seat was still in good order. They both looked at the broken harness and exchanged glances.

She secured herself in his seat and gave him a grateful smile. The harness fit over the curves of her body as she snuggled into the seat. He helped her tighten the straps, not because she needed the help, but because he enjoyed being near her. He was beginning to feel glad he'd run into Kelly Tucker again. Some heartstring told him there was something unfinished here, something he needed to explore.

'Thanks,' she told him. 'You hang on now.'

He grinned at her as he fastened his own seat strap across his waist. It would at least keep him from flying out of the seat completely when they hit turbulence.

'Don't worry,' he quipped. 'I don't plan to leave your side.'

The west wall would be no gentler.

'Hank Jessup has logged more than two hundred eye penetrations,' Ross continued. 'He knows what he's doing,' Ross said.

'I know.'

He and Kelly exchanged glances again, then pressed their heads back against the cushioned seats as they experienced in reverse what had happened going in. The roller coaster still sent his stomach up to his throat and then flattened him in the seat. But he kept a good hold on the metal bar, bracing himself so he wouldn't bump his head. And the ride began to get easier.

Kelly stared at a fixed point on the instrument panel before her as they jounced around. Finally, the turbulence became more moderate and the clouds less angry. Precipitation out their window became intermittent now. Again, the static strands of Kelly's hair flew up and formed a sort of halo about her head, and Ross found himself staring at her. He just wanted to look at her, to drink in every feature and every curve of her athletic, feminine body. He marveled at how she'd changed in the years since he'd last seen her.

They flew between thick cloud layers for a while; then they were out over the ocean again. Ross heard Enrico contact headquarters.

'*Hercules* to Base,' Enrico said.

Wilson's voice came in, sounding far away. 'We have you, *Hercules*. Over.'

After Enrico relayed his data, he listened to Wilson's crackling response.

'Copy. Transmissions are coming in fine,' Wilson's voice said. 'Well done.'

Enrico pressed the transmitter. 'Thanks, Chief. Isaac's turning east at fifteen degrees.'

'Roger,' Wilson responded after a moment's delay. 'We have your readings now. You can return to base.'

'Roger that,' said Enrico. 'See you in a couple of hours.'

He flipped off the radio and jotted some notes in his log book. Out in the Atlantic, the storm moved slowly on its way. As for the passengers in *Hercules*, they were flying in comfort now. Everyone relaxed into quiet chatter against the background hum of the aircraft.

Everyone except Ross, watching those he could see and listening carefully to the other voices, muffled though they were by the hum of the aircraft.

Enrico leaned into the aisle and gave a broad smile in their direction. 'What did the storm chaser's daughter think?'

Kelly laughed a little nervously, smiling back at him. 'Pretty impressive.'

Kelly and Enrico chatted for a while, as Ross leaned his head back and appeared to retreat into private thoughts.

He must have dozed..

What woke him were blips on the radar scope. Neil Devlin, the sandy-haired radar specialist and an old friend, was hunched over his workstation just ahead of Ross. He was reading the position over a headset to Hank in the cockpit.

Rubbing a finger across his chin, Ross frowned at the dense white mass on the scope caused by heavy nearby echo return. Then he told Kelly he needed a stretch and she got up, letting him out. He moved along the aisle to stand next to Neil, bracing himself with his feet apart, one hand on the back of Neil's seat, the other hand through a loop bolted to the overhead.

'What the devil?' Ross growled.

'The storm's changed directions,' said Neil, his voice tight.

They stared at the swirling white mass slowly turning north ten degrees across the radar scope. The eye of the hurricane, where they had been, was visible in the center of the mass like a donut hole.

Ross leaned over and pointed. 'Is it really moving this way?'

'Damn right,' said Neil. This time there was no doubt about what was happening.

Neil barked some information back to Enrico, who grabbed his radio headset and flicked the transmitter switch.

'*Hercules* to Base. Come in.' It was a shouted demand.

Ross's grip on Neil's seat tightened as he watched the rotating bands on the radar scope.

Wilson's voice responded, 'This is Base, *Hercules*. We read you.'

'Revised position for Isaac, sir,' said Enrico.

He called off the new position of the hurricane, the velocity at which it was traveling, the direction, and the wind speed, which Neil confirmed.

There was a pause while they waited.

40

'Roger, *Hercules*. Ground radar verifies your update.'

'It's changed directions, sir,' said Enrico. 'It's growing in strength and it's coming after us.'

'Get the hell out of there,' barked Wilson. 'Get back here as fast as you can.'

'I don't believe this,' Neil muttered as the turbulence got bumpy again. 'Hank, did you get that?' he yelled to the pilot.

'Affirmative. Got it all,' came Hank's voice over the drone of the engine.

'Get us out of here, Hank,' said Neil.

Ross knew the actual storm might be an hour or more in catching them, but heavy winds traveling ahead of the storm could cause a lot of damage.

He wasted no time getting back to his seat beside Kelly as the harness light dinged on. She resettled herself and lifted her sandy brows questioningly as he fastened her in, trying not to show his concern.

The perplexity he felt about the storm's changed direction was sure to show in his face, but he tried to give her an encouraging look.

'We'll be able to outfly the storm, won't we?' she asked in that soft Oklahoma voice that reminded him of home.

'Should do,' said Ross.

She was a scientist, he mused. It would be better to be honest with her.

'But we've got head winds to buck, flying westward, and that storm's now coming from northeast of our position.'

'Wonder what made it change direction,' she murmured, tipping her head to the side and studying all the instruments in front of them. Her lower lip protruded just slightly as she pondered the problem. 'Unless our original readings were wrong.'

Then she looked at Ross, her green eyes wider.

'I'll be fine,' he said, reading her thoughts. There hadn't been time to fix the broken harness. He'd have to hang on tight if they ran into turbulence again.

'Hang on, everybody,' Hank ordered over the intercom. 'We're climbing.'

They managed to find a good cruising altitude, and Hank raced ahead of the storm. Ross sensed the quiet concentration of the entire crew as they flew through rain and clouds doing their jobs. Ross kept one eye on Neil's radar scope. He'd never seen a storm turn so quickly and it started his mind racing. Had there been something wrong with the original prediction? The weather buoys in the ocean would have relayed data later than the data *Hercules* had sent. Wilson would be able to compare it for accuracy.

Out of the corner of his eye he kept tabs on Kelly too, as she systematically recorded temperature, humidity, and pressure. Every inch a professional, he found himself thinking as he smiled inwardly in admiration. Like her dad.

They had to descend sometime, and as they reached nineteen thousand feet, the rain turned to sleet. From where he sat, Ross could see that there was no visibility through the splatter and smear on the forward windows. They were flying on instruments now.

They experienced a few bumps, and Ross hung on to the metal bar, smiling at Kelly to indicate that he wasn't worried.

When they finally broke through the clouds, the sea foamed below with gusts wiping off the tops of waves. They neared the base, and Hank let the wheels down to minimize the turbulence. Ross felt the bump and then the plane leveled out below the stratus.

'Doing okay?' he asked Kelly.

She turned her head to look out the window and gave him a nod. The determination in her serious green eyes made him understand she wouldn't rest until she found out what had gone wrong with the GPS instrument and why the harness straps had failed.

And why they were being chased by a storm they had predicted would go the other way.

3

Inside the Hurricane Center, Wilson Quindry's staff wasted little time analyzing the data and issuing the necessary warnings. People on the coast were told to protect their property. The worst of the storm would pass the tip of Florida and would not come ashore this far north.

An hour later they were all back in civilian clothes in Wilson's office, the global positioning system open on his desk. Enrico DeMarcos had the instrument out of its case and was checking the calibrations in the light from the green hooded lamp on the corner of the desk.

Beside Enrico, Neil Devlin also bent his sandy head over the operation and watched with interest. Ross lounged in a wooden swivel chair situated in front of a long table stacked with papers under a bulletin board. He planted his elbows on his muscular thighs, leaned forward, and folded his hands, watching.

Enrico removed two clips from wires he was testing and squinted at the circuit board.

'There,' he said, picking up a pencil to use

45

as a pointer. The others moved closer to see what he was talking about.

Kelly followed the point of the pencil lead with her eyes and watched as Enrico nudged a chip. It wiggled.

'A loose connection.'

Wilson gave an exasperated expletive. 'You mean that chip wasn't soldered properly?'

Enrico was frowning, his brows almost knotted in his normally sunny, Latin face.

'That's what it looks like to me, sir. But I can't explain it. I examined this instrument carefully before we took it on board.'

'And the chip wasn't loose like this when you looked it over before?' Kelly queried.

'No, definitely not.'

Kelly stood with folded arms, thinking back over the flight. There was tension in the room all around. They had to get to the bottom of this, and fast. The scowl on Wilson's face left no doubt that such mistakes were unacceptable at the Gulf Coast Hurricane Center.

'Could the turbulence have done it?' Ross interjected from where he sat, a dark scrawl on his handsome features. 'Even with the case strapped down, the circuit board might have been jarred, causing the chip to loosen.'

'No, I don't think so,' Enrico said.

He showed them how the circuit board fit

snugly into its case. Kelly agreed. A chip jarring loose seemed impossible unless it hadn't been well soldered in the first place.

It was time to confront the possibility of sabotage. She looked at Enrico; at Neil, whose head was cocked in silent curiosity; and then at Wilson.

'Someone must have pried the chip loose, then replaced the circuit board into the case,' she said grimly.

The same person who had left her the note? she wondered uneasily. She narrowed her eyes. Excluding Wilson, whom she trusted implicitly, any member of the team could have tampered with the GPS including the three men in this room.

She pushed her hair back over her shoulder and lifted her chin.

'I'd like to speak to the director alone, please.'

She waited a moment for the three team members to realize they'd been invited to leave. She watched Ross unfold his limbs and hoist himself up. It annoyed her that he looked just as appealing in loose white cotton shirt and khaki trousers as he had in his flight suit. For a minute his frown seemed to say he wasn't going to leave. But she thrust her chin slightly forward in a stubborn expression that conveyed she meant what she said.

'Thanks, Enrico,' she said, as he laid his instruments on the desk.

Then she tried to give Ross a calm look of appreciation, but found she had a hard time meeting his dark gaze. She could see that he was angry as the three men left the room.

The door closed behind them and Kelly pulled the warning out of her pocket.

'I found this on my chair yesterday.'

Wilson stared at it, then lifted bushy gray brows.

'This is insufferable,' he blustered. 'Who wrote this?'

'You tell me.'

Her eyes met his. 'I'm sorry,' she said. 'I don't mean that literally. I'm sure you have as little idea as I do.'

'Why didn't you tell me about this when it happened?'

She met the authoritative blue eyes peering over his spectacles.

'You had a lot on your mind this morning, remember?'

She lifted her arms in a wide gesture and made a small circle of the room. 'A hurricane threatening Florida. Decisions to be made that would save lives.'

She dropped her arms and appealed to him. 'I thought a petty threat could wait.'

Wilson shook his head and came around

48

his metal desk. The hurricane was moving off, taking the threat of damage out to sea, but they still had a gusty, driving rain to deal with. He looked at the note again and scratched his head, pursing his lips in displeasure.

'I'll investigate this myself,' he said sharply.

'I wish you wouldn't.'

His head snapped up. 'Why not?'

She eased herself onto a corner of his desk and shivered a little in the heavy dampness.

'Because whoever doesn't want me here knows I'll come running to you. Maybe they don't like the fact that your friend's daughter got this plum assignment. I don't know.'

She knew her voice sounded a little shaky, and she took a deep breath to try to bring it under control. She didn't want Wilson to worry about her.

'Well, what does that mean?' he grumbled.

'It means that I'll keep my eyes and ears open, Wilson. But that I'm going to behave as if nothing has happened.'

She tightened her lips and then spoke again. 'I have to keep this job. I have to think of Annie.'

At the mention of her seven-year-old niece, Wilson exhaled a long breath. She knew he cared about his old friend's granddaughter too and wouldn't tolerate any danger coming the little girl's way.

Kelly pressed her lips together for a moment, thinking. Then she leveled her gaze at him. 'I just thought you should know. In case there really is anything to it, you have the evidence.'

'Are you sure you want to treat it this way, Kelly? I won't countenance anything happening to you or Annie.'

She nodded slowly. 'I think it's best. The threats aren't directed at Annie. It seems more a case of professional jealousy. I can stand that kind of heat.'

Wilson removed his glasses and rubbed the bridge of his nose, replacing the glasses in a gesture that Kelly could imagine was a habit of long duration. He blew air out through puffed-up lips.

'You think the loose chip in the GPS was part of this?' he asked briskly.

'Don't you? And the harness straps too.'

He creased all the wrinkles in his forehead. 'The maintenance crew is checking that out now. Someone's going to have hell to pay for that slipup. It could be coincidence. But if it's not, then you are in some kind of danger, Kelly. Your dad would never forgive me if — '

She cut him off with a wave of her hand. 'No, he wouldn't. But nothing is going to happen to me. I think someone on this mission wants to see what I'm made of. Maybe the person doesn't like women on the team. But if I keep my eyes and ears open, I'll find out.'

She tried to give a laugh that came out more of an ironic grunt. 'Who knows? Maybe I've just passed some sort of test.'

She paused and then lowered her voice to convey the finality of her decision. 'I'm not asking off the mission. Maybe this person just wanted to see if I had any guts.'

He grunted. 'Sort of a hazing.'

She nodded more enthusiastically than she felt. 'Something like that.'

He sighed deeply, and she could read the concern and affection in his eyes.

'All right,' he finally gave in. 'If you want to keep a low profile on this, I'll go along with you. But you'll tell me if anything else strange happens, young lady. You hear me?'

She stood up, almost ready to smile. 'I promise.'

She would have reached out to hug her old friend, but was very aware that they weren't on home turf now. She reported to him, and even though she knew that Wilson would do anything in the world for her family, she had to demonstrate her professionalism too. She held out a hand and gave him a strong handshake and a reassuring smile.

'Back to work then,' she said. He gave her his silent agreement, even though she saw a glimmer of uncertainty in his eyes. He walked to the door and opened it for her.

Outside in the map room, her colleagues were bent over charts and maps spread on the huge briefing table, lit by soft fluorescent lights overhead. A few of the clusters of people broke off their conversations and looked up to observe Kelly and Wilson as they emerged from the director's office. But she kept her lips pressed in a straight line, her demeanor neutral.

Her eyes found Ross, who lifted his head from where he leaned over the table on both hands. His glance made her shoulder blades tighten even this far away, but she shifted her gaze forward and strode straight ahead.

She wouldn't dare let anyone know how frayed her nerves had been just a short while ago.

*   *   *

Kelly slid her ID card through the reader at the security desk so that the system would know she was leaving the building. The uniformed guard looked up and nodded to her, marking her name in his log book.

The rain had stopped, leaving large

puddles in the parking lot and a gray sky overhead. She was almost to her car when she heard her name. Ross hurried along the row of cars in his long-legged stride and caught up to her as she was opening her door. She brushed a hand through her straight, limp hair and turned to meet him.

'Hey,' he said.

'Hey, yourself.'

It had been a difficult day, and all she wanted now was to go home, see Annie, and sag onto the sofa. She dropped her eyes to Ross's chest, trying to ignore the fluttering inside her own. She was still noticing things about him she wasn't ready to acknowledge. Like how masculine and appealing he had become.

But his intense gaze forced her to lift her eyes to meet his. The determination in his strong chin told her he was going to pursue something with her, and her heart gave a small lurch at the thought of what that something might be. Damn! She'd never asked for this. It seemed like betrayal, finding herself sexually attracted to the man responsible for her father's death. No! She wouldn't let this happen.

'I just wanted to make sure you're okay.'

He reached up and brushed some damp hair off her forehead. She drew back, turning her head to look down into the bucket seat of her dark blue Mazda Protégé.

'Sure, I'm okay. Thanks for asking.'

She fiddled with her keys, waiting for him to leave.

But he didn't leave. He kept his hulking body beside the car, his arm resting on the car roof. When she looked up, he glanced away into the distance, as if assessing how the storm had moved off. There would be some damage on the beach, most likely. But the storm hadn't come inland, and she didn't feel like talking shop anymore today.

'I just need some rest,' she finally said.

He brought his sharp gaze back again. 'Look, I know you're tired. But I wondered . . . if I could bring by some dinner. I'd like to see Annie.'

Kelly wrinkled her brow. In spite of her fatigue, a twinge of sentimentality made her hesitate to put him off.

'That would be nice for her.'

'She won't remember me. She was a toddler when I saw her last.'

'Yeah.'

Poignant grief welled up in her heart. Had all this been a mistake? Somehow her memories of her father had grown stronger since she'd come here. Annie had come to live with Sherman when her own parents were killed in a car accident. Sherman's older daughter, Noelle, had been Kelly's half-sister from a previous marriage. He'd divorced Helen and married Kelly's mother a few years after Noelle was born.

Helen was still living, but she felt she was too old to take care of a child. So Kelly took care of Annie. It wasn't easy, but Kelly felt a special connection to her niece. Kelly's own mom had died when she was only five, so for most of her life it had been just she and her father. She knew how important it was for Annie to feel secure and loved, and that would always be Kelly's first priority. Helen visited them at Christmas and checked in with them frequently. It was better than having no family at all.

'Yeah, all right. You can come by if you want to.'

His eyes brightened and she chastised herself for responding to his smile of anticipation. What was wrong with her? She needed a quiet evening at home to sort things out. Not a few more hours of dealing with Ross and the uncomfortable feelings he called up in her. She closed her eyes and exhaled a breath, moving to get into the car before she changed her mind.

'Annie likes Chinese,' she said to him before she shut the door.

As she drove off, she saw him standing there, hands in pockets, getting wet in the mist that was turning to drizzle again. She muttered to herself, thinking that she should have kept her distance from him in the first place. He was still the daredevil charmer that she remembered him to be. Maybe she owed him for taking care of her up there today. But a nice dinner and visit with Annie and it would end there. After this they would keep their relationship strictly on a professional footing. After all, she had to get to the bottom of what was going on and who didn't want her there. It might even be Ross, though at the moment her tired mind couldn't fathom that. Daredevil he might be, but sly and manipulative? No, that wasn't Ross King's style. Not at all.

★ ★ ★

Ross ignored the rain as he watched her drive away. The heat Kelly generated in his body was enough to warm his blood. He'd liked the way she'd held on to him up there when she was frightened. It wrenched his gut that someone was trying to hurt her, and that made him determined to stay by her side and protect her.

Not that Kelly Tucker thought she needed

protecting. He'd never seen a braver young woman. Made of the same stuff as her old man, though she wouldn't admit it.

He swore to himself as he started for his own car. He'd read the disapproval and pain in her gorgeous green eyes. She didn't like seeing him there. It reminded her of too many things. It reminded him too — of how tempting she had always been, of how much he'd wanted her back when she was his professor's off-limits daughter.

He felt a surge of anticipation spread through his loins and tried to cool himself off. *Business at hand, old boy,* he admonished himself as he folded his long body into his beige BMW. The leathery smell of the interior was familiar and reassuring. Still, the thought of kissing Kelly Tucker, of splaying her golden hair out on a pillow, made his pulse jump.

But she didn't like him. He was nothing to her but a daredevil playboy. A man who'd gotten her father killed. He shut his eyes as he let the motor idle for a moment, reliving the day of that terrible tornado in Oklahoma. His mind flashed on the scene of their cars lined up on the road, filming and taking measurements as they'd done a thousand times. But it was almost as if Sherman had a death wish that day. He'd told the others to go on; he was going to stay just five more minutes.

And so they'd watched from the van as Sherman finally got into his car and started down the road toward them. Watched as the tornado picked up speed . . .

He opened his eyes and shook his head. He'd replayed that picture so many times he didn't even know if he had it right anymore. He shook his head harder and finally shifted the car into reverse. It wouldn't do any good now. The man was dead.

He found a Chinese restaurant a few blocks from Kelly's apartment complex. The bag was still warm when he parked in front of the white stucco apartment block and walked through an iron gate and into a courtyard. He found the stairwell leading to the second level then turned down a balcony. Finally he located number 203.

Before he knocked, he glanced down the long stretch of balcony to the stairwell at the other end. Below, the damp courtyard was empty. The lack of security bothered him. Kelly was too vulnerable here.

She opened on his second knock, and he smiled. She had changed into a soft, white T-shirt that fell attractively over her round breasts. He didn't let his gaze linger there. There was too much else to gaze at anyway. Her open, honest face; her full, kissable lips. Her face looked a little less worried, and her hair had been brushed and coiled up onto the back of her head with a scarf knotted around it.

'Hi,' she said in that sexy, husky voice.

God, was he going to make it through the evening? This woman made him want to toss the food aside and pull her close right now, sampling her lips with his own.

'Hi,' he grinned. Then he put on his most charming smile. 'Got food.'

'Mmmmm,' she murmured, patting her flat stomach, clad in sturdy, loose-fitting pink shorts. 'We're hungry.'

He stepped into a softly lit room and felt immediately at home. The gold patterned sofa and overstuffed chairs were welcoming, and big burgundy and tan throw pillows offered a homey touch to what must have been a hastily thrown together apartment. A waist-high bookshelf lined the wall to his right.

A large, orange tabby cat with blinking green eyes lay with paws tucked beneath his short-haired body on the braid rug.

'That's Stegmeier,' said Kelly, indicating the cat. 'He came with us from Boulder. He's one of the family.'

'I see.'

Ross crossed the hardwood floor to the dining area and set the paper bag down on a glass-topped dining table. The wood blinds were open to the view of Old Tampa Bay. Kelly padded on bare feet onto the white-tiled kitchen floor and flung open some cabinets.

He lifted the food containers out, calling off what he'd brought. Kelly brought quilted place mats and silverware.

'Sounds great,' she said with a half-smile. 'I'll call Annie.'

From her distracted look, he doubted she'd even heard what he'd said. As she fled to get Annie, he chuckled inwardly. Maybe he bothered her the same way she bothered him. Maybe it wasn't just the old resentment that was beginning to flare up between them. Maybe it was something else.

Still, he frowned, trying to bring his mind back from lust. He needed to keep his head in order to keep her safe. But how could he when the soft movement of her hips and the long, smooth strides of her tanned legs made him want to entangle his limbs with hers.

'Later,' he whispered to himself as he methodically opened the white containers. If he couldn't stop thinking about sex with her, at least he could put it off for a while.

★　★　★

60

Kelly had been unprepared for Ross's sexy presence standing at her front door as if he belonged there. He'd freshened up, and the green, gold, and plum madras shirt and olive twill shorts only emphasized his tanned features, gleaming white smile, and perfect dark hair. She'd felt a tightening across her breasts as his gaze casually appraised her and liked what he saw. It had taken only a second, but already she was trembling again.

This had been a mistake.

She found Annie sprawled on her bed, dressed in her blue-denim overalls and pink and white print T-shirt, and playing with her stuffed horse and turtle. The sandy-haired seven-year-old looked up.

'Is he here? Did he bring the food?'

Kelly grinned. 'Yes, and yes.'

She had already told Annie that Ross was an old friend who used to work with Sherman.

Annie slid off the bed and carefully put the horse and turtle on a rack of similar stuffed animals and came to join Kelly. She suddenly wondered if Ross would recognize some of Sherman's serious looks in the small child. Her even sandy brows over hazel eyes, straight nose, and straight lips were pure Tucker. But she also had the smooth peach complexion of childhood and a dreamy gaze.

She reached for Kelly's hand and they walked down the hall together. Annie was shy, and she pressed against Kelly's side as they walked into the light of the dining room. Ross straightened and smiled.

'Annie, this is Ross King. He knew you when you were just a little kid. Ross, this is Annie.'

Instead of moving toward her, Ross sat down and gave the girl an easy smile. It moved Kelly to see him respond sensitively to her shyness.

'Hello, Annie. I'm pleased to meet you.'

'Go ahead, shake hands with Ross, dear,' Kelly urged her. 'It's all right.'

Annie knew she was never to speak to strangers, and she seemed to have an apprehension of men in particular. So the formal introduction was important.

Annie let go of Kelly and marched across to Ross, holding out a straight arm and offering her hand. They shook. Ross smiled.

'How old are you, Annie?'

'Seven.'

'That's a good age. Do you go to school?'

Annie nodded her head. 'I go to second grade. Mrs. Watson brings me home.'

'Mrs. Watson is our baby-sitter,' said Kelly. 'I drop Annie off in the mornings; then she brings her home and makes dinner for us.'

Ross grinned. 'I guess Mrs. Watson is out of a job tonight.'

'I told her we were having takeout tonight, so she took home the dinner she'd prepared for us.'

Once she saw that Annie and Ross were getting along, Kelly finished setting the table. Stegmeier jumped up on the table to investigate what had arrived in the warm paper bag and had to be set down with a sharp 'No!'

Then they all dove into the food, groaning their satisfaction at the tastes. Annie filled herself up on vegetables, rice, chicken, and shrimp, plus a generous helping of duck sauce applied to cheeks and chin. Stegmeier got lickings from their plates placed on the kitchen floor when they were done.

When they were full to the brim, Kelly cleaned up while Annie washed her face, then entertained Ross with a parade of stuffed animals and an explanation of all their names.

He seemed perfectly relaxed with the little girl, and Kelly wondered how much he'd been around children. She tried to marshal critical thoughts as she washed up in the kitchen and put everything away. But the murmurs of conversation and laughter coming from the living room did not bolster the picture of Ross as the selfish, show-off bachelor she'd expected him to be.

'Time to get that homework done, kiddo,' she said, coming back into the living room. It touched her heart to see Annie enjoying herself so much, she almost hated to break it off.

Ross mocked up a serious look. 'Oh, oh. I'm in trouble, Annie. Keeping you from your homework. I'll get a scolding if you don't run along.'

Annie giggled and crushed some of the stuffed animals to her chest. Kelly saw her niece to her room, picking up the remaining animals as they went.

Before Annie slid into her little desk and took out her writing tablet to practice her letters, she looked at Kelly with round eyes and said softly, 'He's okay.'

'Yeah,' said Kelly, a lump forming in her throat. 'He's okay.'

4

When she returned to the living room, she found Ross sprawled on the sofa, gazing out at the watery scene beyond the dining room table. The orange tabby cat had jumped in his lap and was enjoying being stroked. Ross was pensive, but his look softened when she came into the room.

'We need to talk,' she said, surprised at the words that flew out of her mouth. She stood with hands on hips, feet slightly apart, in battle position.

His eyes swept her frame, again threatening her inward defenses. But he shifted himself up straighter, one arm still sprawled across the back of the sofa. The cat jumped down.

'I know,' he said simply.

She avoided the tempting spot beside him on the comfortable sofa and crossed to the wing chair beside the lamp table. The soft beige lamp shade cast a warm glow over her. Beside Ross, the colorful Tiffany-style lamp shade lit his bright print shirt. Such opposites they were: Ross with his high energy and daring, and his demand to be in control of every situation, and Kelly with her desire for a life that was calm after the storms. Especially after today.

'Where do you want to begin?' she asked.

He drew his dark brows together, concentrating on her. But this time it wasn't the flirtatious, suggestive look she'd caught earlier. This was more serious. But to her surprise, when he spoke, it wasn't about the past.

'I went over the cabin with the flight crew,' he said. 'That strap was definitely monkeyed with.'

She glanced away, not liking the queasiness in her stomach. 'Are you sure it wasn't just worn out?'

'I'm sure. Wilson confirmed how thoroughly the crews double-check everything before and after every flight. Besides, I saw the cut marks myself. If I could find the tool that did it, there would be particles of the fiber on the blade. Any lab could confirm it.'

She pulled her mouth back in a wry smile. 'But you didn't find it.'

He shook his head slowly. 'No. Whoever did that made sure the cutting tool was well hidden afterwards. If we call in the MPs, it should frighten the perpetrator away. That would probably be the safest course.'

She knew he would prefer to catch the saboteur red-handed himself and claim the credit. But she didn't want to draw attention

66

to herself if it could be avoided.

She shook her head. 'I'd rather not. I talked to Wilson, too. Someone doesn't want me here, either from jealousy, or some sexist issue, or something. I can take the heat if that's all it is.'

He narrowed his eyes, causing her a little shiver. 'If that's all it is.'

She lifted her gaze again. 'You think it's more than that?'

She saw the flicker of some reservation in his eyes and felt uneasy.

'Kelly, I need to know everything you know that might be connected to this. Think back over everything that's happened since you arrived here. Let's go over it together slowly. We might think of something together.'

'Why?' she challenged. 'Why are you so interested?'

He gave an impatient little shrug, as if she should know the answer. 'Because it's you the idiot is targeting. It might get nasty. I want to help.'

'Because you owe me something . . . for my father's death.'

There, it was out in the open, or almost. Her adrenaline sped through her veins, and her heart raced. Confrontation wasn't easy, but she knew she had to get past this with him.

He didn't look guilty or try to avoid her eyes. But he didn't speak for a minute, and she thought his lips and jaw tightened just a trace. Finally he spoke with measured words that held a tremor of controlled emotion.

'I was angry at myself after your dad's accident, Kelly.' He stopped and swallowed hard, then went on.

'I still can't explain what happened. Maybe he had car trouble. Maybe he just lost his good judgment until it was too late. I've been sorry about it ever since.'

He leaned forward, his elbows resting on his knees as he stared at the floor and shook his head slowly.

'I've relived that day so many times it's beginning to be a blur in my memory. But I honestly don't think I could have saved him.' A heavy weight hung between them, tangible and uncomfortable. 'I know you haven't forgiven me.'

Kelly realized she was gripping the padded chair arms in a death grip and tried to relax her fingers. She wanted to maintain the upper hand, but his sincerity was throwing her off.

'I don't blame you,' she said. But the harshness of her voice said otherwise.

'You don't?' His voice was doubting.

How to explain the feelings she'd harbored all these years? 'You couldn't tell Dad what to do. I know that. I don't blame you,' she repeated. 'I just think you were reckless, that's all.'

He sat up again, not looking at her. 'We *were* reckless.'

Then he met her gaze, his dark eyes penetrating deep into her soul, reaching into a place she thought was forbidden to anyone. When he spoke, his words were soft, but they sprang across the distance between them as if they were sitting only inches apart.

'Don't you call what we did today reckless?'

She jutted her chin out at the challenge. 'It was a professional assignment, not the same.'

'Come off it, Kelly,' he shot back. 'The media made storm chasing look like a showy hobby. Meanwhile people like your father were gathering scientific data that would help predict storms better. No one knows what causes these storms exactly. The more we learn, the better prepared we make meteorologists. We do it so lives and property can be spared. Surely you realize that or you wouldn't be doing what you are doing.'

Her blood boiled at the direct challenge in his fierce brown eyes. He wasn't going to get off the hook so easily. But she kept her voice low and controlled. She didn't want Annie to hear them fighting.

'You always wanted to be a hero, didn't you? I can see that hasn't changed.'

For a moment they glared at each other across the rug, each one certain of being right and demanding an acknowledgment. He was the first to relent. His look softened, and he frowned.

'We can't undo what we did. We both feel bad about something that happened. We both think we could have prevented it. We didn't. But life goes on, Kelly. I doubt your dad would want us spending six entire years blaming ourselves. There's work to be done. He would want us to do it.'

She turned her head aside, not wanting to take any more of his fierce gaze. 'We are doing it.'

'That's better.'

They gave themselves a minute to breathe; then Ross began again.

'So let's analyze our present problem. I want to know who's making trouble. It seems to be aimed at you, but we don't know that for sure yet. Maybe the person just wants the mission to fail generally.'

'It is aimed at me,' she admitted quietly.

She hadn't planned to tell him about the note she'd shown Wilson, but she somehow couldn't keep it from him.

She dropped her shoulders in resignation

and stood up. 'Stay here. I have to get something.'

She looked in on Annie, to make sure she was doing all right, then stepped across the hall to her shadowy bedroom. Ivory wood blinds opened onto the same bay view as the dining room, and she closed them now, turning on a soft bedside lamp. Then she got the key out of her purse and unlocked the drawer in the small rolltop desk that sat in the corner. She stuffed the note in her pocket and returned to the living room.

She thrust the piece of paper at Ross and then took her seat again. His lips parted in surprise as he read it, and when he looked up, his complexion had darkened. True anger now showed in eyes that were nearly black.

'When did you get this? Where?'

'It was on my chair yesterday.'

'And you didn't tell anyone?' he practically growled.

'I told Wilson. Today, after the flight.'

His lips drew into a straight, gray line. Small muscles in his jaw worked. She was surprised at his display of emotion. Almost as if he had a personal interest in catching the culprit. A suggestion tingled down her spine.

He just stared at her, but she could see his mind working, clicking off possibilities. She continued to explain.

'I didn't want to make a fuss. I figured that was what this sick person probably wanted, for me to go crying to the director.'

'So you risked your neck instead.'

'No more than you or anyone else did,' she returned. 'We all knew the mission had some inherent danger.'

His shoulders relaxed only slightly, but he continued to frown. 'I still don't like it.'

'Why? You think you can make it up to me for what happened to my father?'

He didn't answer, and she felt instantly sorry. Pain shot through his eyes, leaving golden streaks in their brown dark depths.

'Sorry. I didn't mean to snap.'

He got up and moved to the other end of the sofa, near her chair. 'It's all right. You're tired. We're both a little on edge.'

He tried to lighten up the mood. 'Not many people get to see what we saw today, do they?'

'No, that's true.'

He reached over to grasp her hand, rubbing it comfortingly, as if to soothe her nerves. But the contact only jolted her with an electricity that seemed to spark between them no matter what. She tried to ease back, but his grip remained. He wouldn't let her go.

'Ross,' she said a little breathlessly. 'Maybe you'd better go.'

'Yeah,' he said, his voice throbbing with blatant suggestiveness now. 'Maybe I should.'

'We . . . ' She struggled for words. 'Shouldn't spend time together . . . like this, I mean.'

He inched closer, his face so near hers, her cheeks flamed. Her eyes were lowered, but she could see his tempting, beckoning lips. She swayed forward, responding to his looming protective strength. Suddenly she glimpsed what it would be like to lean on a man like this. Didn't every woman want a knight in shining armor to fight off the monsters in her life, to love and protect her?

Dear Lord, what was she thinking? Things were growing far too intimate. Even as her mind formed the thought, he scooped her up in his arms. Then they were both standing on the rug, her face cradled in his hands, his fingers thrust into her hair.

'Like this, you mean?' he groaned softly as his lips came down on hers.

He tasted so heady and masculine, it made her tingle from head to toe. When his lips parted hers, she responded, her knees wobbling as she clung to him. The desire that thrust upward was so startling it threw her completely off balance. But he steadied her against him: against his firm torso, his muscular thighs, and the unabashed desire that made itself felt through his clothing.

The kiss was long and deep, and Kelly felt as if she was hanging on to him for dear life, until he lifted his face and let her breathe. Then she tried to force some thought back into her dizzy head.

'Kelly Tucker,' he said softly, sweetly. 'I've wanted to do that for a long, long time.'

'You have not,' she said hoarsely. Somehow she had to defend herself against this haze of desire sweeping over her.

His hands slid down over her shoulders to her arms. A mellow smile lingered in his warm brown eyes, where she could now examine more closely the small golden flecks. His evenly placed cheekbones and firm, sensual mouth gave her a double dose of charisma, making little storms swirl inside her stomach.

'I am not lying. I wanted to kiss you the first time I ever saw you. But I thought Sherman might not approve.'

Her own lips curved into a grin at that. 'He wouldn't have.'

'There, you see? I was right.'

She pulled back, steadying herself against the waist-high bookshelf.

'And of course, your lab privileges were more important.' She raised an eyebrow in challenge, but it wasn't malicious now.

He exhaled and lifted his hands in surrender. ''Fraid so. Plus I needed his recommendation for a teaching assistantship if I was going to continue with my graduate studies. I had to toe the line.'

'Uh-huh.' She wasn't sure she believed him, but she couldn't blame him.

Still, she quipped, 'Well, there were plenty of other pretty girls to choose from.'

He lifted a hand to touch her cheek. 'Pretty girls, yes. But no special girls. Sherman Tucker's daughter was special. Still is.'

Her heart did a figure eight in her chest, and she nearly closed her eyes to his tender caresses again. But when she put her hands on his chest, she gently pushed him away instead. She knew that if she didn't get him out of her reach, it might be too late. The chemistry between them was sizzling, and she needed time to think. And to rest.

'You'd better go,' she said. 'I'm just too dog tired to talk anymore tonight. I wouldn't be able to think clearly enough to tell you what's happened. Surely nothing more will happen tonight.'

He registered understanding. 'Yeah, you're probably right. Maybe after a good night's sleep.' He looked around the apartment doubtfully and frowned. 'You don't have much security here.'

'A guard is on the premises twenty-four hours.'

She could see in his brooding look that he wasn't satisfied with that. 'I could stay here on the couch,' he suggested.

'It's not necessary.'

She wouldn't tell him that she didn't trust herself with him in the apartment overnight. She looked him in the eye. 'I think I need some time alone.'

'All right,' he said reluctantly. 'But call me if you need me.'

She got him a pad from the kitchen so he could write down his number. Then she saw him to the door and watched him walk down the stairs.

The moist air outside was redolent with the scent of the seaweed washed up on shore nearby. An eerie light cast by the westering sun streaked the sky. The negative ions seemed to feed her spirit, making her unaware that her body had any weight at all. She felt aware of every nerve ending in Ross's body, as if their spirits still mingled as a result of their kiss. Suddenly she wondered if she would sleep at all that night.

5

The next day at the Hurricane Center was spent poring over maps that had tracked the storm. The weather team analyzed reports of the damage and compared them with their predictions. At the end of the day, Wilson Quindry called them all into the briefing room. Kelly noticed how tense everyone was. People spoke in quiet whispers if they spoke at all. Direct eye contact was avoided. They knew they were in for it.

Their predictions about Hurricane Isaac hadn't been good enough. By the time it became apparent that Isaac was going to hit the tip of Florida, it was almost too late. So far, no lives had been reported lost. But it was a close call, too close. And property damage had been severe.

Wilson glowered as he entered the room and everyone went still. Kelly had taken a seat beside Enrico DeMarcos, and noticed that even his eyes weren't laughing now. He stared glumly at the front of the room.

Ross had followed Wilson in and shot Kelly a glance. She almost imagined a trace of irritation in his eyes that there was no seat beside her. On her other side was Johann Amundsen, who sat with arms folded across his chest and knees apart as if he was not about to move.

So Ross strode across the room and turned a chair backward, straddling it, his arms resting on the back. His dark brows drew together in concentration as he watched Wilson.

Wilson surveyed them all grumpily. But his voice wasn't unkind when he spoke, only brisk with concern.

'I don't know what happened up there yesterday, but let me warn you, such mistakes are not acceptable here. I like to think I know the people I've hired, but I'm not infallible.'

He paused a moment for his message to sink in. 'Whoever is screwing up, whether it be intentional or accidental, will be discovered. I'm not trying to sow doubt about your fellow team members. You have to rely on each other in your work, sometimes even for your survival. But other lives are at stake too. We must make accurate predictions and we must make them fast. I have to ask each of you to take responsibility for correcting these mistakes. If anyone here has any suspicions, however slight, I want you to report to me immediately. Your conversations with me will be confidential. They will not be taped. I'm simply asking you to help me figure out what is going wrong before something worse happens. Understood?'

There were murmurs and nods all around. Even one piece of malfunctioning equipment was out of place in this operation. Two were highly suspicious. So had Wilson started an official investigation? Kelly wondered. Perhaps he had alerted the authorities, but told them to keep it quiet. He wanted to flush out the person threatening Kelly himself. Well, so did she.

Her eyes flew to the side of the room, and she just caught the briefest of exchanges between Ross's studied look of noncommittal innocence and Wilson's flash of . . . something. The two men barely glanced at each other and then the look was gone. But something had passed between them.

Kelly narrowed her eyes, considering. Could Ross be helping Wilson behind the scenes? It was certainly possible. But if they both felt protective of her because of their connections to her father, then she wanted to know about it. She felt a ripple of resentment. She didn't need coddling. She wanted to be treated like every other team member. If there was a private investigation going on, then she should be a part of it. Time for Ross and Wilson to lay the cards on the table.

Wilson removed his glasses, wiped them on his shirt, and replaced them on his face. Everyone shifted in their seats.

'Nina has food on at the house,' he said. 'You're all welcome to stop by.'

Kelly lifted her eyebrows speculatively. Beside her Enrico rubbed his stomach. 'Well, at least the recent crisis hasn't put a dent in the Friday evening feeds. It's a tradition.'

'I guess Wilson did tell me his wife cooks up food for the team every Friday. Do you think everyone will show up?'

Enrico gave her an astonished look. 'My dear girl, where there is food, there is hungry man.'

She couldn't help but laugh at him. 'You don't think people are worried that Wilson is angry?'

Enrico's eyes slid toward the door. 'Actually clever of the old man, don't you think? Whoever doesn't show up will look guilty, hmmmm?'

'Unless,' said Kelly, 'the culprit is *hoping* we'll think that and *does* show up.' She was trying to play along with his attempt to lighten the mood, and was surprised to see the humor go out of his eyes. Had she struck some kind of nerve? She glanced away to find Ross hovering over her right shoulder. His eyes sparked, and she felt a flash of annoyance. Enrico looked from one to the

80

other of them, cleared his throat, and got up to leave.

'See you two there,' he said, lifting a hand as he moved away.

Kelly had gotten enough sleep to be able to function today, but not enough to take the edge off all that was bothering her. And one of those things was Ross. He was moving into her life too fast. As if he belonged there. As if he had a right.

Well, just knowing her father didn't give him that right. She was beginning to resent his domineering attitude. She needed all her wits about her to make sure she did her job well. And to stay alert for more trouble.

★   ★   ★

Wilson Quindry's house was located on the west side of the Davis Islands on an inlet in Hillsborough Bay. A redwood deck over-looked floating piers where forty-foot sailing yachts and motor craft were moored.

Kelly and Annie leaned on the railing, looking out at the boats. Several of the owners were clearing branches away and checking for damage from the heavy rains. The dark blue water of the bay still churned from yesterday's turbulence, the mud and sea life kicked up from the bottom not yet having settled back to the sea floor.

'Will we go on a boat sometime?' asked Annie, peering over the lower railing at the activity on the shore below.

Kelly stroked her smooth sandy hair. 'I hope so. Maybe one of our friends will take us.'

Annie turned questioning hazel eyes upward. 'Are these people our friends?'

The question slithered through Kelly like a somber warning. Her urge to protect little Annie was as great as if the child had been her own. Perhaps their survival instinct had drawn them closer, forming a protective shield against a world where accidents happened and people died suddenly. She had to keep Annie safe. Yet she didn't want to instill any more fear in the child. She just wanted her to be careful.

'The people here are not strangers, Annie,' she said thoughtfully, 'but we don't know them all very well yet. You still need to do all those smart things I told you about. Do you remember?'

Annie nodded seriously. 'Yes. I don't go anywhere with anyone unless you know about it. I don't talk to any strangers. I have Mrs. Watson or the teacher call you if I need to talk to you. I keep the phone number in my lunch box.'

Kelly smiled. 'That's right.' She thought for

a moment. 'You just met Wilson Quindry, right? This is his house.'

Annie moved her head up and down.

'You can trust Wilson. He's a very good friend of our family. If you ever need to get ahold of me and can't find me at my work, you talk to Wilson. Will you remember that?'

'I'll remember.'

'Good.'

Most of the weather team had drifted into the house, and conversation was rising in the spacious kitchen to the left of the dining room behind them. Nina Quindry had put out cold cuts, fresh rolls, dips, and chips, and now the hungry men were digging in. In spite of the troubles, spirits had returned to some level of relaxation, and conversation was growing lively.

Kelly remained on the deck, avoiding the crush at the dining room table. Ross hadn't shown up yet in spite of his offer to pick up Kelly and Annie. But she had wanted her own car so that she could leave when she needed to get Annie home to bed.

At that moment, Wilson emerged onto the deck and came over to join them. He carried a bottle of nonalcoholic beer in his hand.

'There you are. Are you having a good time, Annie?' He lowered himself into a reclining lounge chair to talk to her at eye level.

'Yes,' said Annie. 'Aunt Kelly says you're a friend of our family.'

'Why yes,' agreed Wilson. He gave her a smile. 'I am that. I knew your grandfather very well, you know, and your mother too.'

Annie leaned against his knee. 'All right, then I can talk to you.'

Wilson lifted his eyebrows in Kelly's direction. She smiled, but she saw that he understood what had been going on. He patted Annie's back lightly with his big palm.

'You can count on me as a friend if you ever need one, Annie. Your Aunt Kelly is one of my best employees.'

'That's good,' said Annie. 'We're here because of that, aren't we? Because you said Aunt Kelly can work here.'

Annie twisted her body back and forth, reciting what she understood. 'She goes up in an airplane sometimes and helps predict the weather.'

Wilson chuckled. 'Yes, she does.'

He paused, and Kelly thought she read something on his face that told her he wanted to shift the conversation away from this territory. If Annie understood that her grandfather had been killed in a tornado, he didn't want to suggest to her that Kelly was in similar danger.

'Say, after you have something to eat,

would you like to see my pool table? I can show you how to play.'

Annie tilted her head up, examining his round, friendly face. 'I don't know. Is that like a swimming pool?'

'Well, no. But I'll show you after you eat if it's okay with Kelly.'

Wilson's wife, Nina, slid open the screen door and walked out on the deck. She was an attractive woman in her mid-forties, clad in green silk pants and a peasant blouse that flattered her figure. Her medium blond and gray hair was wrapped up in a bun with a colorful green scarf tied around it and trailing down her back. Modest gold jewelry accented her tanned décolletage, wrists, and ears.

'Annie dear, would you like me to fix you a sandwich?'

Annie looked up at Kelly. 'I'm hungry now.'

'You go on in with Nina, then,' said Kelly. 'I'll wait out here for a while.'

'Are you waiting for someone?' queried Annie.

Kelly felt the flush of embarrassment. She wasn't *waiting* for Ross; she just didn't know why he hadn't shown up yet.

'No,' she said. 'But I like the view.'

She was almost glad Ross wasn't here yet. One of the reasons she had come was to give more thought to each of the weather reconnaissance team members she was working with. There had to be a clue as to which of them didn't like her. While these scientists were supposed to share information, she knew only too well how competitive science was; reputations, plum jobs, and research grants hung on what individuals did. At the same time, they needed to work as a team so that the Hurricane Center could do its job. Errors were costly.

A moment later, Max Omari came into sight on the long dock that ran along the shoreline connecting the piers to the end of the point. Weathered steps climbed the shore to the houses set on a small rise like this one. Bent palms and shaggy weeping willows followed the shoreline. Farther up the slope, pines and oaks shaded the houses. It seemed to be an old but affluent community. She knew that Wilson and Nina had bought this house some ten years earlier when Wilson had gotten a teaching job at the University of Tampa.

Omari now turned up the steps leading to the house. Wilson pointed and said, 'Max's yacht down there is the *Angelina*. You can just see her name from here.'

Kelly squinted in the direction Wilson indicated to see a forty-or-so-foot motor yacht with dark blue hull and teak deck. A large cabin with large, open windows sat at the stern. The wheelhouse was forward of that. The name *Angelina* was painted in white letters along the hull near the stern.

'Have you been out in it?' she asked Wilson.

'Hmmm. A couple of times. Omari doesn't entertain much.'

'I didn't know you were neighbors.'

'Max lives alone in that bungalow over there. You can just barely see it among the trees.'

Indeed the house was quite secluded. There had to be a path leading from the house to the pier, but she saw no railing to indicate any steps.

As Omari approached the top of the stairs, Wilson went to greet him. Kelly knew that Omari had worked with her dad at the University of Oklahoma. She decided to try to renew the acquaintance.

Her thoughts were interrupted by the hail of Wilson's administrative assistant, Jean Bradshaw. When Jean saw that her boss was talking with Omari, she spotted Kelly standing alone and came over to join her. A wide smile filled a freckled, oval face. Jean was several inches shorter than Kelly, with shoulder-length springy light-brown hair. At the Hurricane Center, Jean had seemed friendly and efficient, with her freckled nose mostly buried in papers or computer work. Now she grinned a wide smile, her brown eyes sparkling.

'Thank goodness it's Friday, huh?' she said.

'Yeah, and it's been quite the week.'

Jean leaned on the railing. Her compact figure was emphasized by a tight, red-and-white-striped, short-sleeved top with low scooped neck and red denim short shorts. Obviously she had no hesitation about revealing her feminine attributes to this mostly male crowd. Kelly felt a spurt of curiosity about just who Jean was trying to attract. She shouldn't care if Jean made a play for Ross, she told herself. Hadn't she just said she wanted to keep more distance between herself and Ross?

She tried to discipline her ungenerous thoughts by engaging Jean in conversation. She couldn't help but like the girl. Jean had made sure Kelly would call her if she'd needed any help with things when she moved in and unpacked. Well, maybe Jean could help her now, though in a different way. If anyone knew the inside scoop about people Wilson hired, it would be his administrative assistant.

'So how long have you worked for Wilson?' asked Kelly.

'Let's see. It'll be three years now. I started while I was still at the university. It was an exciting place to be, so I stayed on.'

'What did you major in?'

'English.' Jean wrinkled her nose. 'What do I know about science? But I've learned a lot from Wilson and the others.'

Kelly turned around and leaned her elbows on the railing. She was tall enough to do it with ease, her long body stretching to the deck. With some amusement, she compared her appearance to Jean's. Her pleated white slacks allowed her room to move, and her white tennis shoes were a casual contrast to the sexy red sandals on Jean's naked feet. But Kelly had dressed modestly on purpose. She didn't like being ogled by men who were relaxing away from the job, some of them enjoying a beer or two.

'Any aspirations to do graduate studies?'

Jean wrinkled her nose again and shook her head. Then she gave Kelly a conspiratorial look, her voice taking on a sultry quality.

'My aspirations lie in other directions, if you know what I mean.' Her impish grin left nothing to the imagination.

Kelly grinned back. 'So which of these hunks are you after?'

Jean's tanned face turned a shade pinker. 'Neil. He and I have had a few dates. He's got a future, that man. As a radar man, he'll never lack for a job.'

'Ahhh. And does he know what you've got planned for him?'

Jean chuckled and turned around, also leaning against the redwood railing.

'Oh, we'll see. If I decide he's the one, it shouldn't be too hard to get him to pop the question.'

'Doesn't it bother you that he does such a dangerous job?'

Jean shrugged. 'Well, I do worry when he's in the air. Guess I've gotten sort of used to it, though, helping Wilson out when they're up there tracking a storm. Makes me sort of feel like I'm up there too. You know, we're all part of a team and all that.'

'Hmmmm. Yeah, I know. Guess the group is pretty close.'

'For the most part.'

'What do you mean? Are there some who don't cooperate as well? Standoffish, I mean?'

Jean gave a little shrug. 'Oh, I don't know. I have opinions, that's all. But I should let you make up your own mind, shouldn't I?'

'Maybe.'

Jean glanced at Kelly. 'I noticed Ross King following you out to the parking lot the other day. Do you and he, you know, have a thing together?' She winked.

Kelly felt herself blush and forced her voice to remain steady. 'No. We just know each other from a long time ago, that's all. He was my father's student.'

'Oh, yes, I know all about that.'

'You do?'

'Neil told me. Ross and Neil flew together before. Didn't you know? In the Gulf.'

'I didn't know that. 'Course I knew that Ross was a pilot before he took his graduate studies in meteorology. But I didn't know about Neil.'

'Neil was his radar man back then. I don't actually know what they were doing. Very secret. Neil won't tell me.'

'Secret? I thought Ross flew fighter missions.'

'Oh, there was more to it than that. Whatever it was, it was classified.' She made a spooky face and laughed. 'Top secret.'

6

The daring fighter pilot himself made an entrance into the dining room just after Kelly and Jean had piled their plates with sandwich fixings. Their colleagues called out a greeting to Ross and he waved in return. Then he slid in behind Kelly at the table.

'Hmmmm, looks good. I hope you've left some for me.'

'Every man for himself,' she quipped back.

She felt a little tremor as his breath fanned her neck. His hair was still damp and he smelled fresh and clean. His effect on her was unnerving, especially when she wanted to eat. She'd need to move away and sit down in order for the butterflies in her stomach to stop.

'Every woman for herself, it looks like to me,' teased Ross.

For a moment she thought he must have noticed Jean's enticing attire, but when she glanced at him, his eyes were on her full plate. He nodded hello to Jean, but his attention remained with Kelly. In spite of herself, a thread of satisfaction laced through her.

Ross leaned closer, and squeezed her waist with one hand. 'Go find us a place to sit. I'll join you as soon as I've filled my plate.'

Kelly checked and saw that Annie and two other children were settled at the small kitchen table on the other side of the waist-high counter that separated kitchen from dining area. This entire floor of the house was open, with attractive angles leading from one cozy nook to another. Behind them a step led down to the carpeted living room with floor-to-ceiling windows opening onto the deck with the view of the inlet.

She followed Jean into the living room, but taking Ross at his word, Kelly headed for the padded window seat at the far end of the room. Oak shutters were pulled back to expose windowpanes looking out onto dense shrubbery and trees at the side of Wilson's property. Nina lit some lanterns on the deck to give them some outside lighting as the evening drew on, but most of the guests were finding seats in the living room, either on the floor or on the sofas and chairs.

Jean had squeezed herself in between Neil and Johann Amundsen. She was laughing and joking with both of them, her body turned slightly so that when she bent over, her breasts brushed against Neil's arm. From the jovial, slightly flushed expression on the radar man's face, he didn't seem to mind in the least.

Ross cut a swath through the crowded party and came to sit beside Kelly. There was enough room for both of them so that they could angle their knees toward each other and set drinks down on the window ledge behind them.

'Sorry I'm late,' he said. 'I hope you're having a good time.'

'Just fine.'

She wanted to ask him what he'd been doing, but she didn't. Things were far from resolved between them, and she had no claims on his time. And none on his secrets. But what Jean had just said had made her curious. Maybe when they were alone, she could ask him. She had to remember her purpose this evening, to try to pick up cues from any of the assembled group that might help her to understand their individual motives better.

'I was just talking to Jean,' she said casually when she'd eaten enough of her roast beef sandwich to take the edge off her hunger.

'Gossip, no doubt.'

'Something like that.'

He eyed her more seriously, his own sandwich poised in his hands ready for a large bite. 'Just be careful who you get close to,' he warned. 'Especially right now.'

Then he bit into the huge sandwich.

She didn't reply, but she knew what he meant. Her initial hunger satisfied, she slowed down to finish her meal. How could she make friends with anyone when she didn't know who to trust? And why was Ross so determined to play this role of protector?

They finished their sandwiches and returned to the table for dessert. Nina had brought out a cherry torte that looked inviting. Or would have if Kelly's stomach hadn't been so tied in knots. But she dished up a piece to take to Annie at the kitchen table.

There, Nina introduced her to Johann Amundsen's son and the next-door neighbor's daughter, a charming nearly five-year-old with white-gold hair done up in pigtails at the back of her head. Kelly's heart turned over as she saw how quiet and mature Annie looked between the younger girl and the squirming, laughing little boy, food splattered all over his face. The neighbor child squeaked at his antics, while Annie ate her supper like a lady, wide eyes shy, if curious.

So much loss in the little girl's life, thought Kelly with a stab of compassion.

A flash of grief and resentment threatened to weigh Kelly down. Life was so unfair sometimes. It hardly helped that one could look back and say, if only . . .

Like the day her father died. If she'd been there, she would have dragged him out of the way. Why hadn't Ross? Her heart churned at her confused feelings. To look at the way he squatted down and talked to the children, one would think he was Mr. Perfect. The hidden regret she sometimes saw in his eyes ought to tell her that he'd learned things, that he wouldn't make the same mistake twice.

Maybe that was it. Maybe he was so fiercely protective of Kelly because he'd bungled it with his mentor. Was she just a stand-in then for a person Ross had admired and lost? Was he doing penance by trying to assert himself this time and catch a culprit?

'How's everybody doing in here?' came Wilson's jovial voice, interrupting Kelly's introspection.

'If their plates are any indication, I'd say their stomachs are full.'

'Well, that's good.' Wilson leaned down over the table. 'Now, who wants to learn how to play pool?'

'I do, I do,' shouted the boy and slid off his chair.

'Come on, girls, you play too,' Wilson cajoled.

'Girls don't play pool,' taunted the little boy.

'What?' Wilson said, looking aghast. 'They will if they know how.'

He straightened and smiled at Kelly. 'Want to see the rec room?'

'Sure.' She grinned. 'Come on, Annie. Let's go look downstairs.'

Ross followed them all downstairs to the cool basement. Green-shaded lamps suspended from the ceiling lit a sturdy pool table at one end of a dark wood-paneled room. Wilson arranged stools around the table for the kids to sit on while he got down the long, slender cues and demonstrated. Kelly was about to leave them there, thinking that Ross, too, might want to shoot some pool. But he followed her up the stairs.

'Let's take a walk,' he said, grabbing her hand.

They headed to the deck, lit now only by the lanterns, for evening had turned into the beginning of a sultry summer night. There were enough clouds in the sky to mask the three-quarter moon.

They slipped off the deck and started down the stairs to the dock. It wasn't steep, and small lanterns mounted on low posts cast soft yellow pools of light on the steps every few feet. Ross still grasped her hand in his strong warm one, and she was glad of it when they stepped onto the dock in the darkness and she felt the gentle rise and fall of the water beneath.

'Watch your step,' he said.

Hmm, that's what I'm trying to do, she thought.

There was less light here, and not enough moonlight to guide them. A few of the boat slips were lit, but most of the crafts silently bumped against the rubberized sides of their piers, rising and falling on the small crests of the tide's ripples.

'Are we walking anywhere in particular?' asked Kelly. Her nerves had been tingling ever since her hand touched his.

'Perhaps,' he said, leading her in the direction of Max Omari's yacht, the *Angelina*. She was curious about it as well. But when they came abreast of it, she glanced behind them. There wasn't any reason they shouldn't be admiring his boat, but she almost felt as if they were snooping. Actually, she *was* snooping. Trying to piece together what her colleagues' private lives were like.

'A sleek craft,' commented Ross as they stood at the long, pointed bow. The dark windows in the empty cabin at the stern looked almost foreboding.

She didn't know much about boats, but this one looked expensive and well cared for. 'I wonder if he spends a lot of time on it.'

'Somebody does. Look at how shiny the hardware is. He hasn't left it here to rot — that's for sure.'

She glanced up the shore and located the cement steps rising to his bungalow, dark now. He must still be at the party.

'Wilson told me he lives up there,' she said indicating the white stucco cottage half hidden by trees. 'He said Omari doesn't socialize much.'

'Mmm,' was all Ross replied.

'I wonder . . . ' began Kelly.

'What?' His deep voice was warm, near her ear.

'Oh, I just wondered if anyone else on the team lives on this inlet.'

'No, they don't,' said Ross in a quiet voice.

Kelly realized suddenly that Ross was speaking so quietly because water could carry voices a long distance. Even though they weren't trying to hide from anyone, she found herself adopting the same hushed tone.

'How do you know that?'

'I just know.'

She was surprised at his certainty. How would he know where everyone lived? He hadn't been here that long.

They began to hear murmurs coming from farther along the dock, and Kelly's ears pricked. In her tense state, the first thing she thought was that someone might be hurt.

Ross lifted a finger to his lips, then tightened his grip on her hand and led her softly along the floating dock.

The moans grew louder, accompanied by a soft panting of breath. It was very dark at this end of the dock, and Ross stopped, motioning for Kelly to keep still. As their eyes adjusted to the darkness, she finally saw what he was seeing. Two figures seemed to move in the stern of a yacht just two piers ahead of them. Lovers, realized Kelly.

Embarrassed, she started to back away. Ross stood still, looking toward the lovers, and Kelly glanced back. The moon came out from behind some clouds, casting a silvery reflection on a shapely leg poking out from under a trap the lovers had used to cover themselves. Kelly saw the pile of clothing on the deck beside the straining bare foot.

A long, sharp moan cut through the air, almost palpable. Kelly stifled a nervous giggle. She and Ross should get out of there before they embarrassed both themselves and the other couple. He turned at last to follow her away. But she knew who was under that tarp, even if she could only guess who she was with. She'd seen the elegant red sandals on the deck. Jean Bradshaw had caught her man.

She tugged on Ross's hand to pull him along. He caught up with her so fast he almost tripped over her. Now they were both shaking with silent laughter, jostling each other like kids in their haste to get away. When they regained Wilson's steps, Ross didn't lead her upward, but put his finger to his lips once again and pulled her in the other direction along the dock. She moved beside him, feeling like a giddy teenager.

Ross finally stopped where the dock ended. She saw the spark of intimacy in his own dark eyes where the moonlight reflecting off the water glinted in them.

'What are we doing here?' she asked, her heartbeat quickening.

'It seems to be a night for lovers,' he whispered.

She felt a tremor race through her as he pulled her to him, pressing his thighs against hers so that his desire was hard and evident against her. He claimed her lips and opened his mouth wide against her, his tongue lacing hers hungrily. She felt her own response, heated by the balmy night, by Ross's powerful masculinity. It awoke feelings that she realized now had been kept buried as she'd struggled with life's challenges.

But Ross seemed to sweep all that away. His arms clamped her to him, and her own arms returned the embrace desperately. They kissed each other and held each other until the need to be closer, to feel each other closer, became overpowering. Ross loosened her blouse from her slacks and slipped his hands along her heated skin. Then with a groan he swept one hand around her ribs to gently squeeze her breast. Kelly gave a sharp gasp, but tried desperately to pull herself together.

'We can't do this,' she whispered.

'Hmmmm,' was all he said.

But his lips lifted from her burning skin. He nuzzled his head against her neck and they swayed together on the dock, until he must have regained control.

'No,' he finally said, his voice husky with desire. 'We can't do this now. Not here.'

Where? her mind screamed. But she waited until her pounding pulse cooled down. She straightened her clothing and combed her fingers through her hair. Annie mustn't see her looking like some wanton woman. Even if there seemed to be only one bed that her traitorous body and disobedient mind wanted to be in.

He bent and brushed his lips across hers lightly, then wrapped his arm around her waist as if to steady both of them as they made their way back to Wilson's house.

Cool it, Ross tried to tell his overheated body. He'd nearly lost his head back there. He knew Kelly's notions about him were confused. Her father's death still stood between them. Perhaps it always would. Going too fast certainly wouldn't help.

He tried to concentrate on his real job. And ironically her safety had somehow become a part of that. If some sociopath thought he was going to harm a hair on Kelly's head, or on Annie's for that matter, that person was very much mistaken.

As they climbed the steps back to the deck, he made no attempt to hide what would seem apparent when they returned. He didn't mind if people thought he and Kelly had slipped away for a little privacy. In fact that was the perfect cover for what he really had to do.

Finding whoever was interfering with the Hurricane Center's storm predictions, allowing hurricane destruction that could have been avoided, was hurting the state economy through crop failure and weather damage. Ross had been assigned by the Bureau of Land Management to find the saboteur. Now Kelly had become the center of some kind of threat, which didn't bode well. If someone was trying to discredit her, he must have a powerful reason.

Ross would like to think that Kelly was right, that it was just professional jealousy. But that was highly unlikely, given that the sabotage had started before her arrival. No, somehow she represented a threat to the manipulator.

Kelly didn't know about his intelligence training, and he didn't have enough reason to reveal it just yet. His mission here as an investigator was classified. And he didn't want to frighten her by suggesting that she might be at the center of something bigger than she suspected. If she were in danger, it would be better to send her home. That would be the way to keep her safe. Send her away until the errors were traced to their source and his job was done.

But as he looked at her firm chin, the slight upward tilt of her head, and the set of her shoulders as she crossed the deck to the sliding glass doors, he knew she wouldn't leave. And he felt an unfamiliar tug of emotion as he realized he'd miss her if she did.

In the dining room, he picked up a beer and unscrewed the cap. He had tried to put Sherman Tucker's death behind him; tried to accept his part of the responsibility without forgetting that Sherman was doing what he wanted to do. Ross had tried to move on, and had. Until he saw Sherman Tucker's daughter. Saw the accusation in her eyes. And wanted to take her in his arms and kiss that accusation away. Now he had kissed her and he knew it wasn't nearly enough. Her own flushed face told him she'd felt the same.

Kelly wandered over to talk to Nina in the kitchen. The brightness in her eyes was a dead giveaway that something had been kindled there. He left the women to talk and eased over to the stairs going down to the basement rec room. From the sound of masculine voices drifting up the stairs, he guessed that the male guests were engaged in a game of pool below. He tipped back his beer, took a swallow, and then took the stairs downward.

The kids must have gone elsewhere, for they were no longer getting their pool lesson. Instead, Wilson was leaning over the table, about to take a shot. Enrico was leaning on his pool cue, and the tall, quiet Swede, Johann Amundsen, held his cue upright by his side as if standing at stiff, military attention. Omari rested his cue on the table and studied the configuration of the balls on the green felt as if they were part of a scientific experiment. Neil wasn't there, but Ross could guess why.

Wilson sank the seven ball in the left-hand corner pocket, drawing the cue ball down the rail with a backward spin. It knocked the nine ball into the right-hand corner pocket as planned. The game was over.

'Way to go, Wilson,' said Enrico.

'Is good,' pronounced Johann.

'How 'bout another game?' asked Enrico. 'Join us, Ross?'

'Sure,' he said, setting his bottle on a small table at the side of the room.

Playing games together was team building. And he needed to get to know these men very well. To find out whether one of them didn't like having a storm chaser's daughter in their midst.

★ ★ ★

On Saturday morning, Kelly decided she'd spend some time at the base. The GPS failure had unnerved her. True there was nothing she could have done about a loose connection. However, in order to stay on top of things, she thought it was important to put in some extra time. Besides, there were squalls to the south. She might get some practice at scanning thunderstorms.

She promised Annie that they would go to the shopping mall later on, if Annie would come with her to the office this morning.

Annie crossed her arms importantly in front of her and tipped her head to the side, considering Kelly's offer. The wide hazel eyes stared up at her, speculating.

'Hmmm,' Annie finally said, pressing serious lips together. 'Will I get to see how they make the weather?'

Kelly smiled. 'We don't actually make the weather, Annie. But we watch it and then tell the weatherman on TV what we've seen so he can broadcast it for everyone to see.'

Annie's eyebrows lifted as she digested this piece of information. The spark of interest in her eyes touched something in Kelly's heart, but also gave her a sense of trepidation. Annie had never said what she might like to do when she grew up, although she had a great fondness for animals. If she weren't careful, Annie might follow Sherman and Kelly into meteorology. Being a weather forecaster was all right. But a sudden protectiveness made Kelly want to make sure Annie grew up wanting a desk job, nothing dangerous.

'All right, I'll bring Tor Bear and Dogget,' Annie agreed, naming two of her favorite stuffed animals.

'The rest of you stay here,' she told the remainder of the herd that leaned together on the shelf.

Kelly put on jeans and a loose cotton shirt, while Annie came clad in dungarees and blue T-shirt. Traffic was light, and the clouds had departed in the night, so the sun was steaming up the morning already. The heavy humidity and rising temperatures reminded her that this was Florida. One hardly marked the passing of September into October here. A month traditionally thought of as autumn stretched before them with the promise of only slightly shorter, sticky days.

Steamy heat from the pavement of the parking lot rose upward, creating odd mirages of huge pools of water where none existed, and a building that looked distorted as if in a fun house mirror.

Inside, the air temperature was a little more comfortable, and Kelly took Annie through security and up to the second floor. The elevators opened to reveal the weekend shift of meteorologists scanning radar screens and satellite pictures of the earth. Printers hummed as digitized graphs printed out data gathered by weather satellites and beamed back to the base. But after yesterday's flurry, things had settled down to normal, and Kelly passed quickly through the room to her section, nodding to those who looked up.

She turned the corner to find that she wasn't the only one from her team to decide that Saturday was a good day to get caught up on things. Enrico was at a metal desk, hunched over a sheaf of papers, and —

She stopped suddenly. The workstation Johann Amundsen was rising from was her own!

He turned and stopped when he saw her. Enrico glanced up at the same time. His Latin face lit up in a smile of greeting and he rubbed his eyes as if from relief from reading.

'Ah,' said Enrico. 'Two lovely ladies come to brighten our morning.'

'I came to work,' she said in a voice she realized must have sounded somewhat strained.

Johann stood in front of her computer, his hands folded in front of him.

'Good morning,' he said in his formal way. 'I was using your computer just now to see if the image capture software works. Mine seems not to be working.'

Her eyes flew to his workstation. Sure enough, his computer was booted up, the northern lights screen saver dancing across the screen. She tried not to be jittery. What he said sounded plausible.

'And did it work?' she asked Johann.

He nodded. 'Yes. I will reinstall.'

He moved away from her station, and she quickly scanned the area to see if he'd left any suspicious notes behind. Everything looked normal, and her top drawer was still locked. She breathed easier.

She smiled at Enrico. 'I just thought I'd spend some time reviewing procedures. This week taught me I have a lot to learn.'

'I know what you mean.' His sunny expression turned sober. 'These reports, very bad.'

She sighed. 'Yes.'

'Who are the animals?' asked Enrico, stretching his arms over the desk to Annie.

She showed Enrico the stuffed toys, while Kelly took a seat at her computer.

'How would you like it if I showed you some big pictures of the earth taken from a satellite?' Enrico asked Annie with a grin. 'Would you like that?'

Kelly turned around in time to see Annie nod enthusiastically.

'Is it all right, Aunt Kelly?' Enrico asked her.

Kelly smiled. 'It's fine. Stay on this floor, though, unless you tell me.'

Enrico got up from his desk, saluted, and took Annie's hand to go into the bigger room to show her the pictures spread out on the big worktable.

Kelly was immediately absorbed in her work. When she finally leaned back and saw a dim glow of light from Wilson's office, she realized she hadn't even noticed him come in. She stood, stretched, and walked over to check on Annie and Enrico. Her niece was still enraptured with his tour of the map room, so she stepped back and turned toward Wilson's office.

When she knocked on the doorjamb, he looked up from the papers spread on his desk and motioned her in. He hadn't turned on the overhead light, and there weren't any windows in this office, built in the center of the building as it was. Only the desk lamp glared down at the small print on the pages spread out before him. He motioned her into a chair in front of his desk.

'How's it going?' she asked, reading the weariness in his face.

He peered at her through his spectacles and then leaned back in his swivel chair, hands folded over his stomach.

'Sometimes I wonder why I took this job,' he confessed with a sigh.

'You have a lot of responsibility.'

'And getting harder all the time.'

She nodded, sensing he was in the mood to talk.

One hand swiped across the reports on his desk. 'Latest complaints from the governor. Reminding me that the average cost of preparing for a hurricane in the Gulf Coast is fifty million, whether the hurricane strikes or not. The prediction business gets to be more of a political nightmare every day.'

She nodded, sympathizing. 'The potential loss is greater as well, because of population growth in the vulnerable areas.'

'Everyone wants beachfront property. And most of those people have never experienced a major hurricane. They don't want to evacuate under blue sky conditions; they want to hang around until they can actually see and feel the threat.'

'I know what you mean — then it would be too late. People would be trapped in those areas cut off from escape routes.' She glanced at his reports. 'So if we're going to force them to leave, the governor wants to be sure there's really going to be a hit.'

Wilson grunted. 'Something like that. Nobody *wants* a hurricane. The economic losses can be devastating to businesses that have to close down.'

He inhaled a long breath through his nostrils. 'I once viewed this job as a mission to save lives and minimize property damage. Now I'm not so sure.'

A quiver of guilt sliced through her. 'That bad?'

Abruptly he sat forward, got up from his

chair, and moved to close the door. When he sat down again, his blue eyes stared straight at her.

'When we have the potential to be accurate within an acceptable margin, I can accept the responsibility for making the call. But I have to be sure the data I get is accurate.'

Her spine tingled. 'And it's not?'

He shrugged. 'Witness what happened in *Hercules*. The weather officer relays one set of data. Then thirty minutes later, I get a frantic call that the storm has veered suddenly off course in a way I've never seen before. The data we got later from the weather buoys indicated an error in the original data.'

He drew bushy brows together. 'I don't like it that someone up there might have made a mistake.'

Kelly sat up straighter. 'If you think any of this is my fault, please say so. I'll pack up right this minute and look for another assignment. I won't allow my position here to be influenced by our friendship.'

He raised a hand in a calming gesture. 'Now hold on here. I wasn't pointing a finger, and especially not at you. We already established that the GPS failed because of a loose chip. Not your fault. I'm just . . . well, unloading, I guess. It's a habit I developed with your dad. I'm sorry. I shouldn't have burdened you.'

She relaxed her shoulders and leaned forward. 'No, Wilson. You're not burdening me. I just . . . don't want to disappoint you, that's all.'

'And you won't.'

'But someone wants me to.'

He frowned. 'Yes. I'm working on that. If someone is trying to scare you away, I'll have their job. And that's a fact.'

'I just hope we find out who it is before anything else happens.'

He reached across the desk and patted the hand she had rested on the corner.

'Well, we'll pull together, won't we? Straighten out whatever is going on and get these reports as accurate as can be. When I have to make a recommendation to the governor for an evacuation, I'll be on firm ground.'

'I hope so.'

She appreciated Wilson's candor, but she left the office feeling no more reassured. As she came into their work area, she saw that Neil Devlin had joined the little group of Saturday workers and was bent over Johann's computer looking at the screen. Conferring on the reinstallation, no doubt.

She sat down at her terminal and touched

the space bar to send the northern lights of her screen saver away and get back her screen. When she did, her eyes opened wide with shock.

The thick, black letters nearly filled her screen.

FATAL ERROR. GO BACK HOME.

7

'Is this some kind of joke?' Kelly said through gritted teeth.

The shock had paralyzed her at first, but now she slowly leaned back and turned to stare at her colleagues.

Neil looked up curiously and nudged Johann, who turned to see what she was talking about. Enrico had just brought Annie back into their area, and at the tone of her voice he stopped in surprise.

She quickly assessed the expressions on each man's face. Could one of them have done this? She was especially suspicious of Johann, whom she'd caught red-handed at her computer. But the puzzlement on his face displayed no nervousness or guilt, only his usual serious contemplation.

Neil frowned and came closer, a pencil stuck behind his ear. 'Probably an error message. I don't know these machines well enough to help you. Johann, come look at this.'

The tall Swede rolled his chair over to her station and frowned at the glaring letters on the screen. 'What were you doing when the message appeared?' he inquired.

'Nothing,' she snapped. 'I was in Wilson's office and just sat down.'

She tried to calm her reaction. She didn't want Annie to see that she was upset. Enrico led Annie closer, but lifted the little girl up to sit on his desk while he joined the group hovering around the computer. She thought he blocked Annie's view of the hateful words on the screen on purpose, but he might have just taken the only place there was left to stand.

He shook his head. 'You have never seen this message before?' he queried.

'No,' she said, keeping her voice normal. 'This isn't what an error message looks like. Someone had to program it for this oversize print — unless the computer is truly about to fry.'

She allowed just the right touch of sarcasm into her voice while still watching her colleagues. She hated this, having to suspect everyone. But someone had programmed that message. And she'd damn well better find out who.

'Better get our systems manager to check it out,' suggested Neil. 'Jean can arrange it on Monday.'

She thought she read the flicker of some emotion in his eyes when he mentioned her name. Well, she wasn't going to bring up the fact that she and Ross had almost interrupted their tryst last night. But if they wanted to keep their relationship private, they ought to find a better place to make love than on an exposed boat deck.

'Yeah,' she said, still eyeing them all. 'That's what I'll do. I'll mention it to Wilson before I leave.'

They all shook their heads in puzzlement. If one of them was covering up guilt, he was doing a good job of it.

Then Johann leaned forward. 'If you like, I can search for that file. We might be able to locate the date it was created.'

'No,' she said quickly, shifting her weight in front of the keyboard to block his access.

If there was any evidence as to who had been monkeying with her computer, she didn't want anyone removing it.

He nodded and leaned back; then the little group dispersed. She glanced up to see Annie swinging her legs on Enrico's desk.

'Come on, honey. I'll show you what I'm working on.'

She tried to eliminate any tension from her body as she helped Annie down and spent the next half hour showing her what she did. It was good for children to be exposed to various professions, she reasoned. And if

Annie was going to take after Kelly and Sherman, she wanted to be able to steer her into one of the safe, secure jobs. She would never let Annie take it into her head to become a storm chaser. Even though she, herself, had followed in her father's daring footsteps, she liked to think she didn't take unnecessary chances the way Ross and Sherman used to do.

The memory of the broken harness strap sent a shiver of apprehension through her. Even with all the professional precautions in the world, someone had slipped through the net of checks and double-checks to cut that strap.

She set Annie down, deciding that it was time to take her on her promised trip to the shopping mall. They would eat lunch there and browse through the stores. While she was wandering with Annie, maybe she could sort out just why someone on this team considered her such a threat.

She left Annie to play with her animals for a few more minutes while she stuck her head in Wilson's office. He was still frowning over reports, making some penciled notes on a blank sheet of paper.

'Sorry to bother you,' she said.

He sat up and stretched. 'You're never a bother, Kelly. Come in.'

'I'm getting ready to leave. But I just thought you should know, there was an odd error message on my computer when I went back to the terminal after I'd been in here.'

She hated to bring more bad news, and she hated even worse to look incompetent. But there was no way she could have fouled up the computer. She'd been sitting in his office.

He frowned. 'What kind of error message?'

She grimaced. 'Telling me to go home.'

Wilson's face darkened. She knew he wasn't angry at her, but was interpreting the message the same way she had.

'What program were you running before you got the message?' he finally asked.

She shook her head. 'I wasn't. I was closed out of everything except the screen saver when I came in here.'

His scowl got deeper. Then he reached for the phone. 'I'll get Michael in here right away.'

'Do you want me to stay?'

'That won't be necessary. Just fill out one of those green computer problem forms. I'll make sure he gets it and can find out what happened. That's his job.'

Kelly felt a shiver, but she didn't argue. She knew that their systems manager had to keep all the equipment running flawlessly. They couldn't afford any downtime.

'All right. I promised to take Annie to the mall.'

'You deserve it. So does the kid. I'll take care of it.'

Kelly filled out the form as quickly as possible and dropped it on Wilson's desk. She suddenly was desperate for some distraction that had nothing to do with the Gulf Coast Hurricane Center or any of its staff.

★ ★ ★

The West Shore Plaza Shopping Center was just what Kelly needed. She and Annie ate Cajun food at the food court, then wandered in the cool mall. Looking at window displays and wandering in and out of the big department stores provided just the right amount of colorful fantasy to help her relax.

At the toy store, Kelly told Annie she could pick out one thing, and they spent a long while giggling and discussing the possibilities. When they finally made their purchase and left the store, Annie became thoughtful again. After a few minutes of failing to engage her in conversation, Kelly led her to a bench angled across the middle of the mall between two cart vendors.

'What's wrong, honey?'

Annie sighed. 'The game says it has to have

four people to play it. We're only two.'

The serious, round eyes held such a touch of loneliness it wrenched Kelly's heart. She tried to smile brightly.

'Well, there's Mrs. Watson. She would play with us. And we'll just have to invite someone else over for an evening. Would that work?'

Annie observed her with pursed lips. 'Will you ask Ross?'

Kelly's heart bumped. 'Well, I don't know. Why? Do you like him?'

'I guess so. He's not as funny as Enrico. But I think Ross likes *you*.'

Kelly reached an arm around Annie and gave her a hug. 'You'll promise to tell me whether you like my friends or not, won't you? I don't want to get involved with anyone you don't like, ever. Okay?'

Annie looked up at her. 'Are you involved with Ross?'

'No, I'm not.' She considered, wanting to be honest with Annie. 'I like him too, but I don't know if I want to get involved with him.'

Since Annie seemed to understand the concept of 'involved,' Kelly didn't try to talk down to her. 'I don't know if I need a man in our lives right now. What do you think?'

Annie's eyelids dropped a fraction, her sandy eyelashes casting delicate shadows on her smooth cheeks. 'Don't you need someone to take care of you?'

'Well, I don't know. Don't you think I can take care of myself?'

Annie gave a quick shrug. 'You take care of me. So I thought someone should take care of you.'

Kelly's throat tightened.

Simple logic. If only it were that simple in life. Kelly felt a mixture of amusement and tenderness she could hardly explain.

They were still sitting there on the bench watching the passersby and contemplating their next destination when Kelly saw a familiar tall, broad-shouldered figure striding purposefully toward them. She opened her eyes wider in surprise.

It was Ross, with that steady, confident gait of his. He was dressed in tight-fitting jeans and a bright, sexy, turquoise V-necked knit shirt that emphasized his tanned good looks, dark hair, and supreme self-confidence.

As Ross got closer, her eyes were drawn to his perfectly crafted face. She tried hard not to let his good looks influence the way she felt about him. Good looks were only on the surface. The man she chose had to have much more than that. Much more. He would have to be dependable, warmhearted, loving, responsible. Someone she could count on.

Ross smiled when he reached them, and she had to push her criticisms aside for the sake of pleasantries. Never mind the way his eyes melted into hers and lit with pleasure as he saw them both. He grinned at Annie.

'Big day shopping?' he asked.

'Ummm-hmmm,' nodded Annie. 'We bought a game. Want to see it?'

'Sure I do.'

He took a seat on Annie's other side and examined the shiny box Annie showed him.

'Spy Master, huh? We'll have to try this, won't we?'

Over her head he gave Kelly a wink, sending her heart skittering. She looked away. Until things were sorted out, she'd have to avoid being alone with him again. She wasn't immune to contact with those strong arms and sensual lips. Just chemistry, she warned herself. She'd been misled by chemistry a couple of times by guys who'd just wanted a good time. She was determined not to be misled again. She and Ross would work together and that was all. But already her blood was warming up, just from sitting near him.

He looked very seriously at Annie. 'I'll have to get your aunt to invite me over so we can play. What do you think my chances are?'

Kelly felt the flush burn her cheeks as

Annie swiveled her head between them, then said, 'I think your chances are very good.'

In spite of herself, Kelly croaked out loud. 'Annie,' she chided. 'Ross is just being nice. Maybe he doesn't want to play.'

Ross lifted a dark eyebrow and sent a bedroom gaze over the top of Annie's head.

'Oh, but I do.'

Kelly's face warmed further. 'Well, we'll see.'

Ross smiled easily, ruffling Annie's hair, making her giggle.

'I stopped by the base and found out where you two had gone. I thought maybe I'd see if you wanted to take in a matinee. I stopped by the theater complex. You have the choice of a talking goat or a flick about King Arthur.'

'King Arthur,' said Annie, jumping down with excitement.

Ross let his warm gaze settle on Kelly's face. 'How 'bout it?'

She gave a resigned sigh. After all, it wasn't just her day. She had to think of Annie.

'Okay, that would be very nice.'

Annie walked between them holding their hands as they strolled through the mall and out to the parking lot. *Like a family*, Kelly couldn't help but think. A sudden yearning for such a fantasy to be real swelled her heart. That's what a shopping mall was, wasn't it?

she mused. A purveyor of all the shiny, pretty things you could imagine, a place to lose yourself in the fantasy of what life would be like if you wore this dress, drove that car, scented your bathroom with that flowery soap. And the sexy, virile man holding Annie's hand was part of the fantasy too. A hunk to hold you in the night. To make love with under a tropical moon.

Stop it! she commanded her wayward thoughts. She'd come here to think, and all she was succeeding in doing was dream.

8

Ross glanced at Annie to see that she was enthralled by the druids' old magic come to life on the screen. Seeing that upturned face, so reminiscent of her granddad, touched a tender spot in his insides. He'd never thought much about family. But he was changing.

It had started with the war, really. As a fighter pilot in the Gulf, he'd flown secret night missions carrying aerial photographers over enemy territory. He'd also dropped American spies behind enemy lines. He'd gotten shot at and lost some friends. And he'd developed a hatred for megalomaniacs who allowed conditions to escalate to war. Being a man of war had turned him into a man of peace. He'd turned his efforts to working for a better environment, and decided then to learn to make weather models of storms, to help predict what made them happen. That was when he'd met up with Sherman and gone storm chasing.

He glanced over Annie's head at Kelly, wondering if perhaps Sherman would be pleased that he wanted to court his daughter. He faced front again, watching the draped figures on the screen conjure up a spell. Was that really what he wanted? Just looking at Kelly's long, luscious figure stirred desire in his loins, and her inner beauty and her obvious love for her niece had added a tender warmth that invaded his soul. But he couldn't afford to start something he wasn't prepared to follow through on.

He grinned to himself in the darkness. He couldn't believe he was considering the idea of settling down. He only knew that there was something about Kelly's inner flame that beckoned to him. Made him want to know more. Made him want to spend time with her and plumb her depths. Just how he could do that and keep his hands off her he didn't know. But he'd read the caution in her face. She wasn't ready to be pushed. And she was in trouble now — she needed his help, not his passion.

The movie played on, but Ross's mind remained on Kelly. Wilson had told him about the ominous computer message when he'd stopped by the base. Ross was certain it hadn't been her fault. Then whose? He should have been investigating, but he'd made a beeline for the mall because he'd felt an urgency to get to her side first. To make sure she was safe. And he was going to stick by Kelly and Annie for the rest of the evening, whether they wanted him to or not.

After the movie they all agreed they were hungry.

'Burgers on me,' Ross said.

They headed for a specialty burger place and slid into a booth. After studying the menu, he called in their order over the telephone on the wall.

Annie chattered about the movie, and then Ross played tic-tac-toe with her on the napkin until the food came.

'Mmmmm,' he said, eyeing his mushroom burger with melted cheese. 'Just what the doctor ordered.'

'Looks good,' agreed Kelly. She rewarded him with a smile before launching into her burger stacked with thick onions, lettuce, and tomato.

They kept the conversation casual and ate until their stomachs could hold no more. Annie grinned happily at them both, and let Kelly wipe the catsup off her face.

'We'll go pick up your car and then I'll follow you to your place,' Ross said when they had left the restaurant.

He slid his fingers through Kelly's. She didn't pull away, but reached for Annie with her other hand.

If she minded his obvious intent to stick to her like glue, she didn't give any indication.

He liked holding hands with her. She was tall enough that her shoulder almost touched his. From the possessive instinct she aroused in him, he no longer wondered if he was doing this because of Sherman. Or just because it was his job. His job was now an excuse. He wanted to be around her as much as he could.

They walked outside, still hand-in-hand. Widespread clouds in stacked layers had grown intense and dark in the evening sky. Wind rustled in the palm trees lining the boulevard leading out of the parking lot.

'Large-scale disturbance on the way,' murmured Ross, looking skyward.

'Flow of moisture from the southwest,' said Kelly, almost simultaneously. To the north, bright sunlight shone through a thin layer of high cirrostratus that appeared to float above all the other layers.

Ross felt a burst of pleasure that their minds were traveling along the same lines. Together they stared at the patches of puffy, rolling altocumulus with dark, shadowed sides. She was a woman he could really share his life with. A woman not only of incredible sexual allure, but one with a sensitive and intelligent mind that she wanted to put to use.

She seemed to read his thoughts, her

eyelids lowering just slightly. She inhaled the warm, moist evening air as if her body were her own personal barometer, weighing the density of the air overhead. Then she met his gaze steadily, warmth glowing like embers in her green eyes.

'It's mesmerizing, isn't it?' she said. 'The coming of a storm with all its power unleashed. That's what my father loved about it.'

She tilted her head back and let the breeze float over her face, her eyes closed. The powerful electricity flowing between them made him want to seize her face between his hands.

'You feel it too,' he said softly, watching the clouds slowly unfurl across the sky.

The air was charged not only with the tropical disturbance that lay somewhere behind those clouds, but with the tension between them.

'Let's go back to your place,' he said. 'We need to talk.'

She opened her eyes and looked at him, her hair beginning to tangle over her face. But the wariness was back in the green eyes as she opened the car door.

'Okay.'

After stopping to pick up her car at the mall parking lot, they caravanned to her apartment. By the time they'd gotten out of their cars and into her courtyard, the raindrops were tickling their faces. They got inside as distant thunder erupted.

'Just made it,' laughed Kelly, entering and turning on the living room lamps.

Stegmeier rose from his place on the rug and gave them a greeting stretch.

Annie headed for the dining room table to tear open the cellophane wrapping around the new game. The orange cat followed slowly, tail in the air. Kelly glanced at Ross.

'Look, you don't have to stay. It was a lovely afternoon. Thank you.'

He planted himself in the living room, feet spread on the braid rug.

'I think Annie might have something to say about that. We've got to see if this game you bought is any good.'

He saw the points of red flush her cheeks, and hoped that meant she was feeling some of what he was feeling.

'But it takes at least four,' she said.

He lifted his arms, palms up. 'No problem. We'll invite someone to join us. How about I give Neil and Jean a call?'

'No,' Kelly said quickly. 'They might already have plans.'

The embarrassed look on her face told him she was imagining just what kind of plans those might be.

'I'll call Mrs. Watson,' she said hastily and fled for the phone.

★ ★ ★

The baby-sitter might not have been Kelly's first choice for Saturday night company, but the middle-aged woman was a safer bet. Kelly might enjoy Jean and Neil's company, but watching them together might be her undoing. Not that they wouldn't be discreet in front of Annie. It was her own imagination with Ross around that she was worried about. No, Mrs. Watson would provide the safest mix for them.

After an hour of Spy Master, Mrs. Watson volunteered to brew some decaffeinated coffee and then get Annie into her pajamas and read to her before bed.

'Thanks, Mrs. Watson,' said Kelly, getting down the coffee cups.

With Mrs. Watson and Annie occupied in the bedroom, Ross sipped his coffee and leaned back on the sofa. Kelly had sat down on the opposite end, a large throw pillow between them acting as a barrier.

'I need to know some things, Kelly. I hope you won't mind my asking.'

She studied his face. 'Oh? What kind of things?'

He set his cup on the lamp table. She tried

to read his brooding eyes, but they were veiled, shielding whatever might really be on his mind.

'Did your father ever talk to you about his weather modification studies?'

She drew her brows together in puzzlement. 'How do you mean?'

'You know, cloud seeding and that sort of thing, to try to create weather in a certain region that would enhance crop yields. He'd applied for a grant on the subject.'

Kelly didn't answer immediately, but she frowned. Finally she admitted, 'I didn't know he was into weather modification.'

Her annoyance that he seemed to know something about her father that she didn't faded when she took in his concerned expression. There was no arrogance attached to it. He wasn't goading her. So why had he brought it up? She voiced her question.

'I just wondered if you knew anything about it,' he said. His liquid brown eyes gazed at her steadily.

'Why?'

His voice was low and intense. 'Because I'm trying to figure out what someone is so afraid of that they are threatening you.'

She lowered her gaze to her coffee mug. 'You really do believe they're threats, not just coincidences.'

'Fatal error. Go home. I don't like it, Kelly. Someone programmed that error message just for you.'

She gave a shiver and rubbed her arms. The rain was coming down harder now, and she got up to get a thick, crocheted throw to toss across her knees. When she sat down again, she drew her feet up under her.

'You think it's one of the team?'

'I can't prove that. But who else has the access?'

'Wilson's investigating it,' she said. 'Surely the culprit will reveal himself in some way.'

His gaze met hers seriously. 'I hope so. But in the meantime he or she could lash out when you least expect it.'

Kelly considered this. Perhaps her day of relaxation had helped her figure a few things out. 'I don't think so,' she said slowly.

'I think these moves are coldly calculated. The person may be desperate, or afraid, but they're definitely cunning.'

She was trembling a little beneath the soft angora throw as her gaze reached out to Ross's dark, concerned one.

'It's scary, Ross. I have to admit I'm frightened.'

His hand started to reach out to touch her face, but they heard Mrs. Watson coming down the hall and sat apart. Kelly composed herself and let the baby-sitter out, thanking her again.

Mrs. Watson gave her a kindly smile and nodded admiringly toward Ross, who had stood to bid her goodbye.

'Enjoy your evening, both of you,' smiled the middle-aged woman. 'I'll see you Monday morning.'

Kelly didn't miss the admiration in the older woman's eyes. *You're never too old to get a thrill*, thought Kelly with humor. Just an example of how Ross could charm the socks off a woman of any age.

She tiptoed down the hall to check on Annie, who had fallen asleep with the cat curled up beside her. Bending over, Kelly kissed her forehead. The little angel didn't wake up, but stirred in her sleep, her hand falling against the warm, purring cat.

''Night, sweetie,' she whispered. Then she turned out the lamp, leaving only the tiny night light glowing in the electrical outlet.

When she returned to the living room, she saw that Ross had lowered the lights. His shadowy figure was stretched out along one end of the sofa, and she felt a deep yearning spiral upward within her.

She could hardly see his face, but he lifted a hand to draw her nearer. She locked her knees.

'I thought we were going to talk,' she said with a slight croak in her throat.

'We are,' came the guttural response. 'Sit down by me.'

'I . . . I'll think better if I sit on this chair.'

'All right, have it your way.'

She sat down on the chair next to him, but soon realized her mistake. Ross rolled off the sofa onto his knees, sliding his hands along her denim-covered thighs. His lips came down on her knees.

'Can't help myself,' he said, lifting his head to look at her guiltily. 'You do powerful things to me,' he said with such stark honesty that she felt the shock wave of her own arousal.

She might have resisted even so, but something in his sincere, yearning brown eyes made her heart turn over. Some echo of loneliness that resonated within her.

'Kelly,' he groaned, on his knees now, his arms reaching for her waist. 'You don't know how much I want you.'

Her heart hammered wildly, and she felt the shimmer of desire course through her — followed by panic. She couldn't be falling for this man, this storm chaser. It was just stress that made her want to slide down into his arms. Just fear that made her long to lose herself in his caresses.

'We can't,' she whispered, even as he

buried his face in her lap, her own fingers entangling in his thick, dark hair. 'We can't.'

'I know, I know,' he whispered in return. He turned his cheek to rest on her thigh.

A glimmer of a smile lit his eyes and he lifted his head, his hands still on her hips. 'I'm not going to rush you. I won't do anything you don't want me to do.'

Then he stood up, lifting her to her feet as well and guiding her to the couch. 'Just let me hold you,' he said.

She sank down beside him, engulfed in his arms. He didn't try to touch bare skin, just held her in a warm, protective embrace, his head against hers, his breath feathering warmth against her ear.

Damn! This wasn't going to work either. She wanted to turn her face toward his, to breathe in even more of that comforting male scent. She wanted to slide her hand under his shirt to press against his hard chest. And then he was kissing her, long and lovingly, pressing her back against the sofa and stroking his hand upward to cup her breast. Her arms clamped around his strong torso, the throbbing deep within her growing overpowering.

'Oh, Ross,' she finally breathed. 'Why are you doing this?'

He lifted his head, the shadows of his

well-shaped cheekbones and strong brow sending desire coursing through her.

'I can't help myself,' he admitted. 'Don't you feel it, Kelly? I want you, my love. But I won't force you. I don't force myself on anyone.'

She managed to cool the microbursts within her body and put her hands between them.

'On anyone,' she whispered. She pushed against his shoulders to communicate her message.

He backed away, but grilled her face with his gaze. 'You can't tell me you don't want me too.'

She managed to summon up enough resentment to sound off-putting.

'I'm not up for a one-night stand,' she got out.

He backed off a little, but his arm was still cradling her shoulders.

'Kelly Tucker, you listen to me. When I make love to you, it won't be for one night.'

Damn! Why did his voice have to sound so sexy and sincere? He could have any woman he wanted, but instead of the macho daredevil she knew him to be, he sounded more like a wounded puppy.

'Oh?' she answered coolly, smoothing her clothing.

'No,' he said, glowering at her. 'You don't know me very well, if that's what you think.'

She gave a laugh. 'You're right. I don't know you. I just remember all the coeds ogling you on campus when you were a graduate student. How many of them did you leave strewn along the way?'

His frown deepened. 'You don't give a person credit for growing up, do you?'

Her heart still hammered, but more from her effort to defend against his persuasiveness than from passion.

'I'm sure you mean what you say, Ross. It's just that you might change your mind in the morning.'

His gaze continued to heat her face, but the passion in his eyes gave way to resigned acceptance. Humor even tempted the corners of his mouth.

'Have it your way, then. I won't make love to you until I'm sure I won't change my mind in the morning.'

'Oh,' she exclaimed and grasped the throw pillow that had been tossed to her other side. She stuffed it against his chest and stood up.

He followed, raising his hands in defeat. 'Okay, okay, I know when I'm being thrown out.' But he wasn't angry now, he was teasing her.

She straightened. 'Thanks for entertaining

us . . . uh, Annie, I mean.'

She glanced out the window and saw that the rain had slackened. He probably wouldn't get too wet running to his car.

Beside the door, he lifted his hand and laid it on her cheek. Then he kissed her forehead. 'I won't forget where we left off.'

Then he was out the door. She closed it and leaned against it for a while. He'd definitely undone her, and she felt a sob of regret. Perhaps she should have let him stay. Let him carry her away on the wings of passion, if only for one night. At least she would have had that much.

And come to your senses in the morning, a voice in her head taunted. What the hell did she know about Ross King, anyway? How could she know she could trust him? She shook her head, checked the lock on the door, and padded softly down the hall to bed.

★   ★   ★

Ross slid into the BMW and sat watching the rain drizzle across his windshield, waiting for his body to cool and the pain of desire to ease. It took a long time, but he finally was able to think of other things. About how complicated things were getting.

He was getting closer to Kelly than he'd

expected he would. He didn't like hiding anything from her, even though his present investigation demanded secrecy. He hadn't counted on falling for her the moment he saw her. But that was what had happened, wasn't it? The fact that she seemed to be endangered by someone or something going on at the Hurricane Center made it that much worse.

He drummed his fingers on the steering wheel. The only logical reason that he could think of for Kelly being threatened was that she knew enough about her dad's weather modification theory to recognize someone else duplicating those experiments for underhanded reasons. Could the same person also be interfering with weather predictions at the Hurricane Center? If so, why?

He had to think of his mission first. Ross couldn't blow his cover yet, not even with Kelly. Not until he found what he was looking for.

9

On Sunday, Kelly decided to stay home and take it easy. She and Annie baked cookies, then ate them as they watched the rain. Wilson called to see how she was doing. She knew he was being fatherly, and convinced him she was fine. She didn't need anything. Ross called as well, but she let the answering machine pick up. In the afternoon, she exercised indoors, since she couldn't go for a jog. Then she curled up with a book, but she couldn't concentrate very well. She supervised Annie's homework, and then made sandwiches for the next day's lunch. A long, boring day. She was glad when the rain stopped and she could step out on the balcony and watch the sunset.

A layer cake from dark blue-gray to fiery pink stretched across the western sky. Long, smooth fingers of gold and orange, and wisps of creamy white provided the frosting. She almost brought Annie out to see it with her, but didn't want to drag her away from her homework. Annie got to do enough weather watching without being forced to turn her face upward at every change in the sky.

But Kelly recognized the source of her impulse. Sunsets were better when shared. Even so, she didn't return Ross's phone call.

Later that evening, as she sat alone watching the news, stroking Stegmeier's thick orange fur, her mind returned to Ross's question about her father's weather modification studies. She drew her brows together, thinking hard. As a sophomore in college, she hadn't been as attentive to her father's work as she might have been. That was a time of exploring other areas that life had to offer, other possibilities. It wasn't until the following year that she'd changed her major and studied meteorology.

She shook her head, trying to remember. She'd certainly known about cloud seeding for a long time. She couldn't remember when she'd first heard of it. Maybe her dad had mentioned it over the dinner table, but it hadn't held any special significance for her.

Obviously, it had for Sherman, at least if what Ross said was true. Darn it, most of her father's papers were packed away in boxes back in Boulder. There wasn't any way she could go through them now to verify what Ross had said. There might be a few of his papers still in the bottom drawer of the desk. She would have to look.

The weather report came on.

'A cluster of thunderstorms is moving westward,' said the weather announcer, pointing to the animated map behind him. 'These could become the seedlings for a tropical storm. No warnings have been issued yet, but advisories say check weather reports over the next twelve hours. And expect heavy rains.'

Storm warnings sizzled in Kelly's mind. The heavy black cumulonimbus clouds on the weather map definitely pointed to a storm. She shut off the television. She'd better get her rest. It looked like they'd be flying again.

★ ★ ★

When Kelly got to the Hurricane Center Monday morning, things were hopping.

"Morning, Kelly,' chirped Jean between tearing off computer printouts and handing them to Max Omari, who waited patiently at the curved reception counter. 'Have a nice weekend?'

'Hmmmm,' responded Kelly. 'You?'

'Heavenly,' grinned Jean.

Kelly could only imagine. She reaffirmed her opinion that Jean and Neil might have found a Saturday night round of Spy Master with a seven-year-old and a middle-aged baby-sitter a bit slow for their taste.

'Hi, Kelly,' greeted Enrico when she approached her workstation.

'Hi, Enrico. Tracking this storm I see.'

The twenty-four-inch monitors blazed with colored pictures coming in from the satellites. Kelly glanced over at Johann's station where the bright red, yellow, and green on the infrared picture indicated temperature and rainfall in the different parts of the storms coming their way. On the screen next to his, the movement of the storms was being charted on a map that showed the southern Atlantic and the Caribbean.

'How far out is it?' she asked.

'Less than four hundred miles,' said Enrico. 'Up we go.'

He rolled his eyes to the ceiling to indicate that soon they would be in the sky.

Wilson appeared at Kelly's elbow. 'I need you to capture those satellite pictures,' he said. 'We have to forward a file to the Gulf Coast Weather Service.'

'Righto.'

Her spine tingled as she sat down at her computer and logged on.

Wilson turned to address the room. 'Listen up, everyone. Tropical Storm Joseph is bound to be upgraded to hurricane status within the hour. You're going up as soon as *Hercules* is finished fueling. Ground crew is out there checking now. Be ready to leave at oh-nine-hundred.'

The excitement was palpable as the weather scientists scurried to take readings and chart the path of the storm they were tracking. Kelly felt it herself, the thread of excitement tinged with danger. *Especially for you*, a voice in the back of her mind warned, but she pushed the thought aside. She wasn't going to run away from a job she'd come there to do.

Her palms were sweating a little. *Don't mess this up*, she told herself. She studied each of the satellite pictures as they came in. When a shot was clear and provided a valuable picture of what was going on up there, she carefully saved it to a file on her hard drive.

She was so intent on getting it right that she didn't even see when Ross came in. Rather, she felt his presence a few feet from her.

As she saved the last picture, she glanced at him out of the corner of her eye. He was in his flight suit already, standing with hands on hips watching the red blur crawl across Johann's screen. Kelly copied the files to a disk and stood up. She had to brush close to him to get to Wilson's office.

His hand almost imperceptibly caressed hers, and a spark leapt between them. She couldn't fool herself into thinking it was static electricity. It was electricity, all right, but a far more personal kind.

She handed the disk to Wilson, and turned to leave, intending to get into her flight suit.

'Kelly, I was considering keeping you here this time.'

She halted at the door and craned her head around. 'What?'

He came out from behind his desk. 'It might be safer for you here on the ground.'

She straightened, her lips in a firm line.

'I'm not asking to be coddled. I take the same risks as the rest of the team.'

'I know you wouldn't shirk your job, Kelly. But something's not right here and I'm afraid someone wants you out of the picture. I can't risk sending you up there when I don't know what's going to happen next.'

She didn't have time to talk to him about what Ross had said regarding her father's experiments. That would have to wait. So she just said, 'These little incidents, if they really are threats, have not been confined to *Hercules*.'

He exhaled through his nostrils. 'I know that. But I feel safer combatting what I can see and hear on the ground without the

148

complications of sending you into a hurricane too.'

She tried to keep her voice level and reasonable. 'Thanks, Wilson, but I can't accept. I've got to hold up my end on the team.' She shrugged. 'What would the others think?'

'Nothing, except that I'd assigned you to track the storm at your desk.'

'That wasn't what I was hired to do.'

They glared stubbornly at each other for another heartbeat, and she had the distinct feeling the Wilson and her father might have locked horns similarly in the past. At the same time, she felt the concern emanating from him, and she knew it was her safety he was thinking of.

'Sorry,' she said softly, taking a step toward him, as if trying to make him understand. 'I have to go.'

She felt her heart clench, and in that moment, she almost felt that her daddy stood in the room with them. He would understand.

★ ★ ★

The team dashed out through the rain and up the metal boarding ramp steps, Ross right behind Kelly. In the gangway, they got rid of their ponchos and then moved forward to take their seats. As she slid into hers, Ross bent to check all the straps.

'Looks good,' he said. His eyes were warm and reassuring.

She examined the fastenings on her workstation. She hated being paranoid, but it was safer to do her own check than to find out too late something else had been missed by the ground crew. She felt the little spiral of nerves and the adrenaline start to kick in.

Ross took his seat. The length and breadth of him so close to her only added to her racing pulse. His smile was meant to comfort. Instead it lit a warm flame within her that was starting to become familiar.

'Everything all right?'

'I think so,' she said.

After takeoff, Hank let them move around the cabin. She and Ross were watching the radar screen over Neil's shoulder when the plane was buffeted by an updraft before Hank could tell them to get to their seats. Kelly was pitched backward and into Ross's embrace. For a brief second she clung to the muscular arms about her waist, engulfed in his willing protection.

'You okay?' he said into her ear.

'Mm-hmmm.'

They balanced themselves against the

cabinets and overhead loops, then took a few rolling steps to their seats to get into their harnesses.

Dark clouds streaked by as they sat taking pressure and wind speed readings. Kelly felt the giddy flip-flop of her insides as the plane bounced, but not the sheer terror she'd experienced before. Still, perspiration broke out on her forehead as she concentrated, and she sensed that everyone was feeling the same tension.

Suddenly a plume of flame shot from one of the engines on her side of the plane, and her entire mouth went dry before she could speak. At the same moment, the plane was hit by wild turbulence. With one hand she clung to the arm of her seat, with the other to the workbench in front of her. All thought stopped, the fear was so great.

Distantly, she heard someone shout, 'Fire in engine three.'

The plane struggled in eyewall winds of 125 miles per hour. They hit another updraft, followed in a few seconds by a lesser downdraft. But all she could do was stare at the flame shooting into the clouds outside.

Ross gripped her hand. Cabinet doors flew open somewhere behind them, and she heard the rustle and clatter of supplies being dumped on the floor. The plane plummeted.

Kelly closed her eyes, certain she was going to die but willing it not to be so. Her only clear sensation was of her cold hand being squeezed by Ross's big, strong one.

Finally the plane penetrated the eyewall and righted itself. In another second, they had leveled out. For a few moments no one breathed. Ross still gripped Kelly's hand and her heart still knocked at her ribs. Then around them, voices erupted.

'Got it out,' she heard the copilot say.

The fire extinguishing mechanism in the engines must have worked. Thank God.

Ross turned to her, and the intensity with which they looked into each other's eyes was so immense, it was as if their very thoughts were melding. In his gaze she read his determination not to lose her, no matter what. The realization made her head ring. He cared for her; she couldn't doubt it any longer. Even if she didn't quite know why.

As the tension in the cabin eased, they finally got up from their seats to help put things back in order.

'Bumpy ride,' joked Enrico.

'It never gets any easier,' said Johann as the two men closed one cabinet door after another and checked the latches.

Max Omari sat stoically in his seat, monitoring the data that was coming into his computer terminal. But she saw that his face looked haggard and green. He glanced up at her as she passed.

'Everything all right?' he asked in his soft, reserved voice.

'Yes.' She tried to give him a smile. 'Just shaken, that's all.'

He nodded somberly. 'I understand. It is always quite frightening.'

'Why do you do it?' she asked, suddenly curious as to why a man his age would continue to ride into storms that one day might kill them all.

He looked out at the calm, smooth air and the clouds surrounding the eye and spoke in a curiously amused tonc.

'Death does not scare me. Whatever will be, will be. What matters is what you accomplish before that. If you are not afraid to die, you do not mind some risks. Every time you beat the Grim Reaper, you have won another day.'

He turned his bespectacled face up to her with a smile that unnerved her. Max Omari was a strange man. She wondered what kind of relationship he'd had with her father. When there was time, she would try to get to know him better.

At the moment there was work to do. She didn't look out at the beautiful, calm eye any more than she needed to. It was only a reminder that swirling around them were immensely powerful rain-filled clouds, bent by the earth's rotation into the deadly circular motion that destroyed. Hard to understand that this wild, driving force was a fact of nature. It killed and claimed property when it smashed ashore. No one could prevent a hurricane. But they could try to plot its course.

They finished gathering all the data they needed inside the eye. When it was time to fly through the eyewall again, an even bigger knot formed in Kelly's stomach.

Ross double-checked her fastenings. With his handsome face hovering near hers, she gave way to the aching thought that if they survived this, she wouldn't hold back any longer. She would give herself to him in celebration of life and joy. Just let them live and she swore she would seize the day.

As if thinking the same thing, Ross's dark eyes bore into hers, flashing with the sensuous thrill of danger, but more than that, with flames of passion. His eyes grazed her face, a hint of pleasure lifting the corners of his lips. Then his gaze burned from her lips down her torso, following the path of his hands as they felt along her harness. When they reached her breasts they lingered there.

Then with one more burning look into her face, Ross sat back and strapped on his own harness.

Kelly trembled. If they had been anywhere else, she would have pressed her mouth to his. She wanted him. She wanted his long, firm body over hers, kissing away all her fears, caressing her with promises of a future.

The stubby plane punched through the opposite side of the storm while Kelly held on and tried to quell her fear. She tried to be resigned like Max Omari, to believe in destiny. It seemed to her that the bumpy ride was not quite as terrifying as before.

Gradually they came out of the storm, traveling fast enough to leave the rain-soaked clouds behind them. Looking out her window, she stared down into paradise — lush green islands bordered by impossible shades of blue water. Yachts anchored near docks that led to peaked-roof mansions. Creature comforts Hurricane Joseph had not yet threatened. Her heart still knocked at her ribs, and Ross wrapped his arm around hers, bringing her hand up to his lips.

He leaned toward her so that only she would hear his words.

'When I realized we weren't going to crash today, I was thankful I was going to live another day to look at you.'

The sincerity in his dark brown eyes made her melt. He had inched his way into her heart and lodged himself there.

But for how long? the suspicious voice inside her wondered.

Even with her doubts, the memory of his kiss was too explosive to deny. She wanted him too much. Maybe giving in to the passion would purge her of this craziness. After a night together, maybe she'd be able to think more clearly. It was a justification, at least, for the way her breasts ached to be touched by him, to feel his searing lips . . .

With a conscious effort, Kelly pulled her hand away and brought her mind back to the immediate problem. They had their readings and were heading back to base. Now they just had to hope that they'd given Wilson what he needed to make the call.

★ ★ ★

But it wasn't going to be so easy. The cluster of thunderstorms they had first spotted headed this way had produced another tropical storm, Katrin. The Hurricane Center was frantic with activity. Kelly stood and watched the satellite transmissions in trepidation as Katrin turned northward. Sixty-mile-an-hour winds swirling toward Cuba.

Johann pointed his finger at the green blob that was the hurricane they'd just been in.

'At least we know Joseph will weaken.'

As they tracked both Hurricane Joseph and Tropical Storm Katrin, adrenaline kept Kelly sharply alert. It was crucial that they accurately predict if and when Katrin would become a full-blown hurricane. As the pressure rose, her feelings for Ross seemed to intensify. She felt his electric presence even when he was across the room. It was as if they had crossed some sort of boundary up there. He was a part of her in a way she could not explain. And yet it frightened her that it was happening so fast.

Several times she felt a small tingle at the back of her head, as if she were being watched. Each time she turned, but caught no one staring at her. She was jumpy, suspicious of everything. She bit her lip, angry at herself. This was no way to get the job done.

At lunchtime, Kelly went alone to the cafeteria in the basement. She wanted to clear her head, and for that she needed distance from Ross. The hum of lunchtime conversation and the glaring lights behind the steam tables were reassuring in their bland familiarity. She slid a tray along, choosing fish and cole slaw, then stopping to fill a paper cup with ice and water.

In the lunchroom, she saw Max and Johann by the window. Deciding to make the most of the opportunity, she walked over to their table.

'Mind if I join you?' she asked.

'No, please,' said Johann, pulling out a chair for her.

Max went on cutting his liver and onions, while Johann swallowed his coffee. Outside the rain was now coming down in sheets.

'In for a long day,' commented Johann.

'Yeah, I suppose,' agreed Kelly. She tried to smile pleasantly. 'But then, that's what we're here for.'

'Ya,' said Johann.

He finished his coffee and set the cup down. Kelly saw that his plate had been scraped clean, and he didn't look as if he was going to stay around to talk. She smiled and dug into her fish, noting that Max wasn't far enough along with his meal to abandon her.

Johann stood up. 'If you will excuse me, I must get back.'

'Sure, see you,' said Kelly.

Max waved a fork.

For a minute Kelly ate quietly, trying to decide how to start a conversation. The man in front of her looked harmless enough, bookish and dedicated to his work, but at the moment, everyone was on her suspect list. And if Max or anyone else had some sick reason for trying to frighten her away, she needed to dig to find it.

She cleared her throat then set down her fork.

'I remember my father saying you were students together,' she began.

Max nodded, continuing to chew and swallow without looking up. 'Yes, yes. We did graduate work together. Then when I returned years later, we were in the same department. I remember you too, though you probably didn't notice me.'

'You taught physics, wasn't it?'

He rewarded her with a darting glance of his murky gray eyes. 'Yes, that was it. So you do remember.'

She shrugged. 'I wasn't as attentive to my dad's work back then. There was so much else to do. But I know I met all his colleagues.'

'Yes.'

He didn't seem inclined to be illuminating, so Kelly forged onward.

'Did you ever work in the lab with him? On his experiments, I mean. He was into things like, well . . . weather modification. To try to increase crop yield.'

There was the slightest hesitation in the

movement of knife and fork as he cut the next bite. But he lifted his shoulders and dropped them in a small shrug.

'Yes, Sherman was always looking forward. And very successfully, too, if I remember correctly.'

'How do you mean?'

He raised his eyes to hers. 'The grants. Being in line for department head.' He lowered his graying eyebrows. 'I'm sorry. He never got the chance.'

'Thanks.'

She ate another bite of her fish and stared vaguely at the lunchtime crowd. It was funny; down here, away from the workroom, she didn't have that odd feeling that anyone was staring at her. Well, Ross wasn't there. Maybe it was just his suggestive gazes that produced the tingling between her shoulder blades.

She returned her attention to the man across from her.

'Were you and my father . . . close?'

Max wiped his lips and looked up at last. He seemed to consider the question. Then he gave his head a little shake.

'We were professional colleagues. I'm sorry I didn't know him well. But he had many friends.'

'Yes,' said Kelly thoughtfully. 'He did have that.'

*   *   *

To their horror, by the middle of the afternoon it became apparent that their predictions that Joseph would weaken proved false. Joseph grew in size and strength and headed for land.

Wilson and the team gathered before the largest of the monitors bringing in the satellite transmissions.

'It's the Fujiwhara effect,' Wilson said grimly.

On the satellite transmissions the storms approached each other. Hurricane Joseph appeared to be chasing Katrin.

'Have we received confirmation that the Keys are being evacuated?' Wilson asked.

Neil handed him the latest telex. 'Confirmation in, sir. Evacuations in progress now. We just got off the phone with the governor's office. State patrol and sheriff's office are coordinating preparations from Key West all the way in to Key Largo.'

Wilson watched the transmission closely. All the scientists appeared fascinated but grim as they watched the murky, spinning storms slowly crawl across the monitors.

'I've only seen this once,' murmured Neil, coming to stand beside Kelly. 'Quite the picture.'

161

Ross and Enrico stared at data coming over the computers, recording wind speed, temperature, and pressure. They rapidly ripped off printouts and handed them to Wilson.

Joseph seemed to have lifted northward, passing over Katrin, while within the next hour Katrin slowed and turned.

Wilson eyed the monitor and studied the readings.

On the screen before them the dance began. Kelly realized she was holding her breath as the storms rotated around each other.

'They are stirring the ocean into a witches' brew,' said Enrico.

Ross ripped off the last report, handed it to Wilson, and then stood just behind Kelly, watching the unique images beamed in on the monitor.

'Just like two figure skaters approaching each other on the ice,' Ross said quietly. 'Just as they are about to pass, they'll grab hands and spin around one another.'

His hands pressed against her waist.

Kelly watched the two storms glide across churning ocean and then, just as Ross described, they began to swirl vigorously around in one big circle, outstretched tentacles of cloud joined between them.

'Like ice dancers,' she heard herself whisper.

Kelly's pulse throbbed with the threat of the storms and the crackling tension in the room. She wasn't sure how long they stood there. Finally Wilson spoke. There appeared to be relief in his voice.

'Katrin's losing wind speed,' he said quietly. 'It looks like she's weakening.'

The swirling dancers on the monitors separated. They would have to track Hurricane Joseph as it threatened the Florida Keys. And wait breathlessly to see if it was going to strike land.

10

Windman considered himself a clever scientist if not a brilliant one. That he was passed over for promotions in the last few years when storm chasing was just coming to the public's attention had grated on him. His true competence as a meteorologist had never been fully acknowledged, and he had never striven for a position of leadership.

Some of his previous employers had intimated that his communication skills were lacking. They did not say it directly, but it was implied that he sometimes rubbed people the wrong way. But he was not unhappy being consigned to the technical side of things. In fact, it had now become useful.

True, he had never been recognized for his work the way that showman Sherman Tucker was. And the storm chaser's daughter had benefitted from her father's reputation. It would be too easy for her to stop him now.

Windman deeply resented those to whom success came too easily. Life had not always been easy for him. But his revenge was close at hand. To have Sherman Tucker's daughter right underfoot was not only irksome, it was dangerous. If anyone could figure out what he was up to, it was she. She and that nosy storm modeler, Ross King. Just like his mentor was that one. He'd heard King had been a daring hero in the Gulf. Now he was here to make his mark as a hurricane hunter.

No, these things were not to his liking. Windman must take further measures to ensure nothing would stand in the way of his plans.

★ ★ ★

Ross confronted Wilson across the director's desk. Spread between them were glossy prints of satellite images, white blobs gradually turning into a swirl of clouds and finally building into the storm they'd flown into that morning. Ross frowned at the pictures, so key to predicting how the storm was developing and which way it was going.

'Fortunately, the automatic backup tape also collected these,' said Wilson.

'So what you're telling me,' said Ross with a scowl, 'is that Kelly's captures either never got made or were erased before she thought she saved them to this disk.'

'That's right,' said Wilson.

Ross folded his arms, legs spread in front of Wilson's desk.

'You're certain she did everything correctly,' said Ross, hating himself for having to ask.

'The girl isn't dull-witted. I'm going to call her in here in a few minutes and ask her, but I know what she'll say.'

Ross's lips curved downward. Time to level with Wilson. 'She doesn't yet know my real assignment here. If you don't mind, I'd rather be the one to tell her, alone.'

Ross felt an unfamiliar sense of embarrassment at having to reveal anything of his personal life. But when Wilson lifted his eyebrows in response, there was no judgment in his sharp blue eyes.

'Like that, is it? I thought you two were getting along awfully well last Friday night at my house.' Wilson smiled briefly. 'Look, I wouldn't have expected you to tell her what you're doing here. I'm cooperating with the Bureau of Land Management because I want my operation to get a clean bill of health, but it's your investigation. I'm only interested in your relationship with Kelly for two reasons.'

'And what are those?'

Wilson took off his glasses and wiped them on his shirttail, then replaced them.

'First of all, I owe it to her father. Kelly's an adult — of course, she can do what she wants. But I warn you, I don't want to see her hurt.'

'I don't intend to hurt her,' Ross said quickly. 'If her father were alive, I would tell him the same thing.'

'Good. Then the second reason is that I need to understand why these mistakes are all pointing to her. I don't think she's making them. Do you have any reason to believe I'm wrong?'

'No, sir. I've been watching her. She knows what she's doing. I checked her record at the National Center for Atmospheric Research in Boulder. She had top reviews there. No chance that she's the bungler.'

'Very well. Then we've got to find out who is.'

Ross studied the older man. 'So you agree she has to be told about the investigation.'

Wilson sighed, came out from behind his desk, and stood facing a large chart on the wall.

'If she's the target, she needs to help us.'

'How do you mean 'help us'? Surely you don't mean putting her in danger?'

'No. In fact I tried to keep her out of danger. She wouldn't hear of it.'

Ross stared unseeing straight ahead of him. It was the first time in his life when professional duty and personal feelings had ever come into conflict, and he was startled by the change.

He clenched his jaw. He didn't want anything to change the loving acceptance he'd seen in those glorious eyes of hers today. All day, as busy as they were, whenever their eyes had met, something new had passed between them. She was going to let him in, and he felt a deep satisfaction at that prospect.

But now she was going to have to learn that he was there at the Hurricane Center under what she might consider false pretenses. It had taken a long time to overcome her feelings about his part in the day her father had died. Now he would have to tell Kelly he hadn't been honest with her. How could he do that? He tightened his lips, thinking about how angry she would be.

He finally focused on Wilson again. 'If you'll let me tell her, sir, I'll do it tonight.'

'Good. Then tomorrow I'm going to have to find things for her to do that don't put us at risk. These satellite images were crucial. If I'd left it solely to her, they would never have been forwarded to the weather services around the region.'

Wilson lifted a hand. 'I'm not blaming her. But I can't take any more chances.'

'I understand,' said Ross.

Ross found Kelly at her computer, a look of puzzlement on her face.

'Hey,' he said.

'Hey, yourself,' she replied, but she didn't take her eyes off the screen.

She wrinkled her brow even more. 'That's strange.'

'What is?'

'Those satellite images I captured this morning.' She sat up slowly, realization beginning to dawn on her. 'They aren't here.'

Ross closed his eyes and let his breath out slowly. 'I know.'

She remained silent for a heartbeat. 'How do you know?'

'Kelly, there are some things you need to know. We need to talk.'

She didn't even look at him but sat staring at the blank directory where her files should have been. It was as if she were contemplating the deep water she was in and what to do about it.

But she was so still and so silent it worried Ross. 'Kelly?'

Then in one flurry of movement, she sprang out of her chair and charged into Wilson's office, nearly colliding with the man at his door. She pushed past him, like an onrushing Greek Fury, the other two men following in her wake.

She spied the satellite images on his desk and tossed them to the side, one by one.

'Where is it?' she mumbled.

'Where's what?' asked Ross, coming to stand close behind her.

But the anger flashing in her eyes held no hint of hysteria. Only recrimination and a flare of determination.

'The disk,' she said, pawing through the pictures. 'I have to check the disk.'

'Kelly, stop,' said Ross.

He reached to grasp her hands and pull her arms around toward him.

'The disk is empty,' he said, forcing her to look at him. 'You don't have to look for it.'

Then he saw the tears start to brim and her lips start to tremble. His heart cracked with what the strain was doing to her. In spite of Wilson standing a few discreet feet away from them, Ross encircled Kelly with his arms and pressed her to him.

'Don't cry, honey. It's all right.'

He heard her sob once, but her fists clenched and she pounded them against his chest.

'It's not all right. Someone is doing these things to me on purpose. I have to find out who.'

'I know, I know,' Ross said softly.

Gently, he pressed his hand against her shoulders, pulling her in close. He rocked with her until she got herself under control.

In a minute she stepped back, swiping at her eyes with the back of her hand. Then she tossed her head, sending her long, blond hair flying over her shoulder.

'I'm sorry,' she said. 'I shouldn't have reacted that way.'

Wilson came toward his desk again. 'It's all right, Kelly. We understand.'

She blinked and sniffed for a moment; then she looked from one to the other of them.

Oh no, thought Ross. *Here it comes*. He spoke first, trying to allay the reaction he knew would explode any minute now.

'Kelly, I've been working with Wilson trying to get to the bottom of matters. I wanted to tell you, but I couldn't.'

Again her head swiveled back and forth between them. Then her liquid green eyes fixed on his face.

'Oh?'

He cleared his throat. He hadn't wanted to do this in front of anyone else, but it seemed he had no choice.

'That's what I wanted to talk about. Alone. I was going to explain it all tonight.'

He saw her jaw tense, her lips pull into a

straight line. 'Explain what?'

He lifted his hands defenselessly. 'What I'm doing here.'

Her sexy eyelids lowered, but it wasn't an invitation. She had grown wary, curling up inside herself in that way she had when she needed to draw up a shield between herself and the rest of the world.

'I thought you were here to study hurricanes, like the rest of us.'

She glanced swiftly at Wilson, then backed away to lean on the front edge of Wilson's desk, crossing her arms in front of her.

'Oh, I see. It's something more than that. Well, this wouldn't be the first time I've been left out of a departmental plan. Why have you suddenly decided to let me in on it now? Casting the dog a bone?'

Ross took a step closer but was stopped by her flashing eyes.

'Kelly, it's not like that.'

Her expression cast daggers at them both. Wilson suddenly found a stack of papers on his side table very interesting. *Just as well*, Ross thought. This was between Kelly and him. At the same time Wilson was trapped in the room. He was part of it, and he couldn't just leave. But it couldn't have become more awkward.

'Look, Kelly. There's an explanation. I was

sent here by the Bureau of Land Management to investigate why the rate of error in this place had suddenly skyrocketed.'

'Oh, I see.' She stared him down. 'Well, you were always doing something special that the rest of us only heard about later. It was like that when you were a flashy graduate student, too, wasn't it? You seduced the professors into giving you the plum assistantships so you could show off.'

'Dammit, Kelly, no! Stop it. This assignment has nothing to do with that. Stop letting your emotions do your thinking for you. We're all on the same side here.'

That silenced her. But her look said he would pay for his accusations later.

They all took a moment to get their tempers under control. Then Kelly spoke, her voice remarkably even.

'I just wish you'd told me from the start, that's all.'

Ross could think of nothing to say but he knew the expression on his face must have been pleading. He was reaching for her across a chasm that had just begun to close. *Trust me*, he wanted to whisper in her ear. But he knew he hadn't earned it.

Wilson cleared his throat. 'It's my fault.'

They both looked at him.

'I knew that for Ross to carry out an

investigation, it would have to be secret. I agreed that no one on the staff could know about it.'

'Even me?' Kelly challenged, eyeing him levelly.

Wilson's face reddened. 'Only for policy's sake. It isn't that we didn't trust you, Kelly. You should know that.'

She didn't argue. 'I understand,' she said. But it was spoken with professional formality.

'I can't prove it yet,' Ross tried to explain, 'but whoever is interfering with our predictions may have some megalomaniac ideas about also trying to influence the weather. He or she is very probably irrational. All the more reason to keep it quiet that someone is officially hunting for him.'

Wilson joined the argument now. 'You see, Kelly, if we push the perpetrator too far, he may become dangerous. He's already threatened you. I will not see you placed in any more danger.'

'Oh,' she said with arched eyebrows. 'And how will you prevent that? Lock me in a cell?'

Ross read the exasperation on Wilson's face. Well, Kelly was the sort of woman it was easy to get exasperated with. She was so damn strong. She just had to butt heads with life.

Wilson gave a sigh. 'I'm not sure. Just try

to make sure that you don't expose yourself to danger, for one thing. And look out for Annie.'

Now fierce defenses blazed in Kelly's eyes. 'You don't think this madman has anything against Annie, do you?'

Wilson exchanged a look with Ross. 'We can't overlook that possibility. We don't know what the man wants, whether he's got a personal agenda or some kind of financial motive to disrupt weather predictions.'

Kelly became more serious. 'I see.'

Wilson circled around behind his desk and grasped the chair with both hands.

'Ross has connections with federal agencies. We've done background checks. Now we're going to have to investigate people's financial records.'

'Like find out who needs money and whether anyone who works here is spending a lot more than his or her salary would seem to justify.'

'Right.'

Kelly turned her gaze to Ross again, but her examination was distant, as if she were assessing him in this new light. As a private investigator for a state government agency. It tore at his gut that she was pulling away from him, closing her heart slowly but surely.

'Kelly, let me see you home. I want to talk

about this some more.'

She went rigid. 'That really won't be necessary. Now that I've been warned, I'll take extra precautions.'

Wilson interrupted. 'I'd like to hire some protection for you, Kelly. I have access to a security firm that I'd like to contact.'

'You mean keep me under surveillance.'

'Not surveillance. Protection.'

'Oh.' Her tone left no doubt what she thought of the distinction. 'By all means, do whatever you think best.' With that she spun around and moved toward the door. Just before exiting, she stopped, her hand resting on the door frame, and turned to look at Wilson.

'By the way. I'm sorry about the blank disk. I should have checked it before I gave it to you. I guess I was in too much of a rush to get ready for the flight.'

Wilson waved her apology away.

'Not your fault. If the files had nothing in them, there was nothing to put on the disk. I've got Michael looking into it now. We're going to give you a new computer. There's a possibility that whoever is up to these tricks programmed your computer to malfunction. We'll switch yours with an identical one while Michael goes over yours.'

She nodded. 'Thanks. I'd better go get

Annie before the storm gets any worse.'

She didn't look back as she left Wilson's office. The wind was beginning to shriek around the outside of the building, a reminder of what they were up against. All along the coast, owners would be boarding up their houses and securing property against the battering that would surely come.

She was feeling pretty battered herself. She headed for the locker room to splash cold water on her face. But even that failed to cool off her burning cheeks. Damn! She hated that she had shown her reaction. But she was just so shocked that Ross had been keeping a secret from her. At the moment the fact that it was a professional secret didn't seem to matter. She couldn't help but be angry. And she would have expected Wilson to level with her as well.

When she returned to her desk, she didn't speak to anyone. People seemed to read her mood and left her alone.

An hour later, Kelly dialed her baby-sitter's phone number. 'Mrs. Watson? It's Kelly. I'm going to pick up Annie. No, you don't need to go. You've heard the weather reports? Good. Be careful. It's getting pretty mean.'

She hung up, put on her rain poncho, and headed for the elevator. The footsteps behind her told her Ross was catching up to her. She wanted the elevator doors to close in his face, but he slipped on before they did.

She tried to move back, but the close quarters of the car placed him right next to her. Neither of them spoke, given the other passengers present, and as soon as the doors dinged open and everyone spilled out onto the first floor, she sped ahead.

'Kelly, wait up. I'm coming with you.'

'Why?' She didn't break stride or look his way.

'Because I want to. It's a mess out there. Let me drive.'

'I'm just going to pick up Annie and get something to eat.'

'I know that. At least let me drive.'

She hesitated. At rush hour in the rain, traffic would be in a snarl. She hated to surrender control to Ross, but she also needed to get to the school quickly. Her old car wasn't the best in weather like this. Ross's BMW would be safer.

'All right,' she said. 'We'll take your car.'

She followed him through the rain to his car and slid in. He didn't waste any time, nor did he speak as he pulled out. She gave directions to the school, then clenched the handle fixed above the door on her side.

Soon they were pulling up beside a low, pink, cinder-block building, and Kelly got out and ran in. Annie was with the other children standing just inside the doors waiting for their rides. She spied her niece sitting close to a little boy her age. The two of them were cross-legged, bent over a book spread between them.

A feeling of warmth uncurled inside Kelly. It pleased her to see that Annie had found a friend. She would have to find out who he was.

'Hello, Kelly.' It was Sylvia Black, Annie's teacher. She was a striking young woman with short-cropped dark hair, dressed in a loose purple dress with scarves trailing at the waist.

'Annie,' she called. 'Your aunt is here.'

Sylvia smiled at Kelly. 'That's Jonathan Whitaker. They played together at recess today. I think there's a friendship budding.'

'That's nice,' said Kelly.

She hoped ruefully that Annie was better at picking her friends than her aunt was.

She reached down to take Annie's hand. 'Did you have a good day at school today?'

Annie smiled shyly at Sylvia and nodded to Kelly. 'Yes. I got a hundred on spelling.'

Kelly brightened. 'Great.'

She glanced at Sylvia. 'I was afraid we were going to make you wait. Traffic was a jam.'

'Not a problem. I stay until the last one

leaves.' Sylvia looked out at the low, dark clouds. 'Are we in for a bad one? I heard the Keys are being evacuated.'

Kelly tried not to sound alarming. 'Hard to tell. If the storm hits cold air over land, it will weaken. Best to be prepared though. Do you live inland?'

Sylvia nodded.

'Good. There might be a little flooding.'

She didn't say any more, too unnerved by the inaccurate predictions they had suffered lately and her own humiliating part in them.

Sylvia waved goodbye and then turned back to the other waiting children. As they left, Kelly couldn't help but take a good look at the school building. The solid old cinder blocks looked as if they could withstand a gale.

Ross had the car doors opened, so Annie got in back. As soon as her door was shut, Kelly slid in front.

'Hi, Annie,' said Ross.

'Hello.'

'Put on your seat belt, honey.'

He started to lean between the bucket seats to reach around to help Annie, but Kelly stopped him.

'I'll get it.'

Then she realized her mistake. She had to

lean toward Ross to get between the seats. He still had his body sideways and didn't move. She tried to ignore the rush of desire that his nearness sparked. Her body was in full combat with her mind, which was swirling with the revelations back at the base. She still felt the sting of resentment at Ross's secrecy about his mission. How could she trust his reasons for getting close to her? How could she understand his motives?

Ross seemed to be thinking as he let the car idle. Then he spoke his thoughts aloud.

'The beaches are already experiencing storm surges,' he said, referring to the high waves that leveled the protective sand dunes and swamped the land behind them. 'Everywhere along the bay, water levels will rise. Your apartment is too close to the shore.'

Kelly fastened her own seatbelt and slid her gaze to Ross. 'We're one story up,' she said, though she knew it was a weak argument.

'You'll be safer at the base,' he said, signaling and pulling into the traffic.

'There could be flooding there too,' she said.

'I know. But the base is more prepared. And the building is more solidly built than your stucco. I'm taking you there.'

It wasn't a question; it was a statement.

Kelly knew he was thinking of their safety, but it still grated on her.

'Wilson needs us anyway,' he added by way of argument. 'We're going to have to keep an eye on how those two storms travel.'

Wilson doesn't need me, Kelly wanted to say. *All I bring is trouble*. But she had to think of Annie. If there was going to be flooding, she'd rather have Annie with her, even if it meant spending the night bunked down somewhere in a sleeping bag at the base. She turned to her niece in the backseat.

'What do you think, Annie? Would you like to come to the base with us?'

Her golden eyes became round orbs. 'Can I? Can I see the pictures of the hurricane?'

Ross turned to grin at the little girl. 'I'll show you how I make a computer model.'

He flashed a questioning look at Kelly. 'That is, if it's all right with your aunt.'

The strict, disciplinary aunt who isn't any fun, thought Kelly resentfully. Now he was going to charm the socks off Annie. She felt her jaw tighten. If he thought he was going to get to her through Annie, he had another think coming. But she smoothed her features to smile at her niece.

'All right. You can see the computer models. But you'll have to do your homework too.'

Annie fairly bounced in her seat. 'If the hurricane comes, school will be closed tomorrow anyway. I'll have time to get my homework done.'

Two *against* one, thought Kelly.

11

Wilson stood in the center of their horseshoe work space. 'Hurricane Joseph is expected to come inland at twenty-one hundred hours.'

The team members exchanged glances. They all knew that meant they'd camp there for the rest of the night.

'No problem, boss,' Neil said. 'How about chow? Any chance we can get the cafeteria to make us some sandwiches?'

'I sent Jean to take care of that. Anyone with family who needs them at home has my permission to go. But I'd like to keep as many hands here as I can get.'

No one spoke.

'Good,' said Wilson, with an appreciative look. 'The second floor is being set up with cots. We can work in shifts. After Jean brings up the sandwiches, she can see to the arrangements.'

As the rest of the team dispersed to call their families, Kelly fell in step with Wilson.

'Why don't I go help Jean?' she said quietly.

She didn't want to admit her paranoia that everything she touched seemed to mess up. But she came from strong, practical roots.

She'd rather be put to work where it was really needed.

Wilson seemed to be following her line of thinking. She read the grim, apologetic look in his eyes as if he didn't like that it had to be this way.

'All right. You go help Jean. I'll keep an eye on Annie. She can use my big table if she has homework to do. With this work overload, Michael probably won't get time to make the computer switch until tomorrow.'

'Then it's better if I do something useful,' she said.

She sensed Wilson's satisfaction with her judgment. He put a hand on her shoulder and gave it a light squeeze.

'I appreciate that attitude.'

She stopped by Ross's computer station to tell Annie where she was going. The little girl was on a chair beside him, engrossed in the colored storm model assembling on his screen. *Starting 'em young,* she thought. It was all well and good that Annie's generation was growing up computer literate. But Kelly was concerned about teaching Annie other survival skills as well. Like how to deal with arrogant, virile males.

'Annie, I'm going to help Wilson's assistant, Jean, get ready for the evening. You can stay here and help Ross for a while. Then

I want you to go into Wilson's office and work on your homework. He said you could work on his big table. Isn't that nice of him?'

Annie dragged her eyes away from the twisting, spiraling model.

'Okay,' said Annie. 'How long will you be gone?'

'I'll check back in a half hour.'

Annie turned her attention to the computer screen again. 'How do you know the color of the storm?' she asked Ross.

Kelly backed away as his smoothly modulated voice patiently explained how the data was sent to the computer by the weather buoys out in the ocean, and she went to find Jean. She ran into Neil coming from the elevators.

'If you're looking for Jean, she just went downstairs.'

Kelly looked at the elevator indicator and saw that the one Jean must have taken was sinking to the basement. The other elevators were on the first floor.

'Thanks. Faster to take the stairs.'

She hauled open the door to the stairway that served as a fire escape and then let it shut behind her. The echo in the enclosed stairwell was a little eerie. *Don't get paranoid*, she chided herself, and grasping the metal railing, she hurried downward. Just after turning on the next landing, she heard footsteps above her. Out of curiosity, she lifted her head to see who else had grown tired of waiting for the elevators and was taking the stairs. But the footsteps stopped. She waited for a door to open and the person to let it swing shut behind him.

No sound at all. She held her breath. Then she let it out and continued downward, more softly, gripping the railing tightly as she went. She heard the steps again.

Rounding the landing between the first floor and the basement, she stopped again. The footsteps above her stopped as well.

She had half a mind to turn around and climb upward to confront whoever was playing games with her. But the fear of being trapped in the stairwell with an unknown pursuer made her palms sweat. She fled down the remaining steps with a clattering and flung open the bottom door with relief. With the unlocked door at hand, her courage returned. She let the door slam in front of her without passing through it; then she crouched beside the stairs to wait for whoever was following her to come down the stairs and go out the door.

She held her breath, straining her ears to hear someone breathing above her. A step. Two steps. She pressed back against the cement stairs, willing the person not to turn around and see her.

Seconds passed and no one came. She held herself rigid, her muscles beginning to ache in the cramped position. Slowly, she turned her head upward, trying to see. She barely caught a glimpse of a hand wrapped around the railing above her. Then a scuffle of movement. The footsteps made no attempt at being quiet. But they were heading away.

Her pursuer had not fallen for the trap. Or he had not wanted to go through the door to the basement corridor and be seen. She rose as the footsteps climbed upward. She heard the first-floor door squeak open and then shut.

She was alone.

Cautiously, she took a step toward the door that she knew was unlocked. Still, she squinted upward in case she was being toyed with in the same way she'd tried to trick her pursuer.

But no one rushed down the stairs. In the next minute, she was through the door and in the basement corridor. Voices drifted from the cafeteria, and in another moment, a couple of people sauntered across the hall.

She realized she was shaking. Someone had followed her into that stairwell — she was sure of it. She hugged herself to try to stop trembling and walked onward toward the comforting voices and movements of people, trying to think who had seen her take that stairwell.

Neil! Some of the others had heard her say she was coming to find Jean, but Neil had been the only person in the elevator lobby when she'd taken the stairs.

It didn't make sense. What could Neil possibly have against her? She began to wonder about those background checks Ross had been doing. When they had a minute alone, she needed to find out if there was anything screwy about the innocent-looking radar specialist.

She found Jean in the kitchen wrapping sandwiches being prepared by one of the chefs. Since the cafeteria wasn't normally open for dinner, she must have found someone still working there in preparation for tomorrow's lunch.

'Hi,' she said to Jean, resting her hand on a stainless steel work counter.

'Hi,' smiled Jean. 'Come to help?'

'Yeah, I thought I'd do something useful.' *For a change*, she almost added, then stopped her tongue. 'I can help you carry that.'

'That would be great. Chef Jeremiah, here, prepared two sandwiches apiece. Hungry men up there.' Jean gave a little growl.

Kelly tried to smile at the humor, even though she suspected that Jean's boyfriend had just tried to frighten her out of her wits on the stairwell.

She took the box of sandwiches, while Jean picked up a large square box filled with apples, potato chips, and corn chips.

'We'll be back for the drinks and cookies,' Jean told Jeremiah as the two women started off with the food.

They hefted their load to the elevators, and Kelly gave the stairwell a suspicious glance. She pressed the elevator button with her elbow, then rested her box against the wall.

'You staying too?' Kelly asked Jean.

The assistant shrugged her shapely shoulders. 'I'll miss my workout at the gym. But the boss needs me here.'

'Yeah. I told Wilson I'd help you with the cots too. If you don't mind.'

Jean widened her brown eyes. 'Sure, if you're not busy.'

'No problem.'

She didn't want to tell the gossipy assistant exactly why she was doing manual labor instead of looking at satellite scans.

They got on the elevator and it started to whine upward. This was the perfect opportunity to question Jean about Neil. She was phrasing her question in her mind, when Jean glanced at the floor indicator.

'Oops. We forgot to press two. Oh well, guess we go for a ride.' Jean laughed.

Good, thought Kelly, balancing her box of sandwiches on the side railing. More time to think of a quick way to get Jean's take on Neil. How long had they known each other? How well did she know him?

She and Jean smiled companionably at each other, and Kelly struggled to keep any tension out of her expression.

She opened her mouth to speak, when suddenly the elevator seemed to sink from under them and then came to a jolting stop.

'What . . . ?' sputtered Jean with impatience.

They both glanced at the indicator. The third floor light was lit, but the doors weren't opening.

Jean pressed on the buttons. Several of them. Then all of them, one at a time. The elevator didn't budge.

Kelly placed the box of sandwiches on the floor. 'Are we stuck?'

'Looks like it,' said Jean.

She tried not to look panicked, but Kelly could see the fright in her eyes.

Kelly moved over to the control panel. When she pushed the red alarm button, they heard the manual ring sound above and below them.

'Someone will come,' Kelly said. She tried to give Jean a reassuring smile.

But Kelly didn't feel reassured. Building fear threatened the logical assumption that this was just a mechanical failure. Either that or the electricity in the building had just gone out. They still had light inside their little box, for the emergency overhead light was battery powered. But the fluorescent ceiling light no longer bathed them with its brightness.

They pressed the alarm button again and again.

'Maybe we should try yelling,' suggested Jean.

Kelly nodded. 'One, two, three.'

Then they both bellowed upward simultaneously. 'Hey, help us. We're trapped in here . . . '

When they ran out of steam, they stopped. They heard someone pounding on the outer doors above their heads. A muffled voice called down to them.

'We're down here,' called Kelly.

Then there was some banging below. She and Jean took turns shouting until it seemed they'd conveyed their position. The voices outside stopped, but she felt a little better. Help was on the way.

Both women sank to the floor.

'Hungry?' asked Kelly, trying to joke away the tension they both felt. It was claustrophobic being shut up in there, but they'd be out soon.

'So how long have you known Neil?' she asked Jean.

She knew the question would distract Jean, but she also knew it caught her off guard. So she had time to watch her reaction.

But if she expected a flush of nervousness, an expression of guilt or subtle malice, none came. Jean blinked at her, looking as if she was trying to relax.

'Um, about a year, I guess. I met him when he started working here. Why?'

'Just curious,' said Kelly. 'Something to talk about to pass the time until someone gets us out of here.'

'Yeah.'

Jean's gaze floated up toward the ceiling as if speculating whether or not they were going to have to climb out.

Kelly kept her talking about Neil. 'Does he have any family?'

Jean brought her gaze back to Kelly. Then her eyes turned soft, as if she enjoyed talking about the man she loved.

'He has a little boy with his ex-wife. I've never met him, though I want to.'

That surprised Kelly. 'I didn't know he had a child.'

'Yeah, it's been tough on him, having to pay alimony and child support.'

'Doesn't the ex work?' asked Kelly.

'Yeah. But I guess they had money problems going into the marriage. I think they split up because of that. They lost money in some wild scheme. Investment in a pleasure boat that sank, literally. Got their friends to invest in it too. Neil's been trying to pay them back. It's why he's always looking for extra jobs to do to pick up some extra money.'

'Sorry to hear that. I didn't know.'

Jean shrugged. 'We all have our problems, don't we?'

Kelly's mind chewed on that. A man who had financial difficulties might be bought by someone who wanted him to perform some sort of sabotage. Or did he have some bigger, wilder scheme afoot to generate additional income? She needed to learn just what kind of 'extra jobs' Neil was engaged in.

The pounding below interrupted them. In a few minutes the doors were forced open, letting in blessed light and air. The elevator car was only a few feet above the floor. Kelly's heart pounded when Ross leaned in to reach for her.

'You all right?'

His face had a fiercely determined look as if he were ready to battle the person responsible.

'Yeah,' she said, her pulse pounding in relief that they were set free. 'But another few minutes and the sandwiches would have been history.'

Ross scooped her into his arms and helped her down, clamping his arms tightly around her. Over his shoulder she saw a workman in overalls reach in to assist Jean. Where was Neil?

Jean brushed herself off and then pointed to the boxes of food. The workman hoisted them down. Finally, Ross let Kelly go.

'What happened?' he demanded.

She shrugged, bending down to pick up the box of sandwiches. But Ross intervened and lifted it up himself.

'I don't know. We got on and Jean forgot to push two. So the elevator went all the way to three. It sort of lurched out from under our feet, then stopped.'

Ross glared darkly. Then he spoke to the overalled workman helping Jean with her box of fruit and potato chips.

'When was the last time these elevators were inspected?' he barked out his question.

The man shrugged. 'Get inspected every

three months,' he said without urgency. 'But you know, they're old. They go out sometimes. It happens.'

'Well, please let us know what caused the mechanical failure. Mr. Quindry wants to know. Got that?'

'Yes, sir. I'll tell Mr. Quindry if I find anything.'

'Good.'

They started down the hall, and Kelly spoke in a low voice. 'You don't think someone stopped it between floors on purpose, do you? How could they? And why?'

His look was still brooding as they headed for the workroom. 'That's what I'd like to know.'

She hesitated. She considered telling him about the intruder on the stairwell, but Jean would hear her, and might run and tell Neil she suspected him. Besides, she didn't want to capitulate to Ross that way, him and his secret investigation. She would just see what she could find out on her own for a while.

Even so, she was acutely aware of the relief she'd felt when he'd lifted her down in his arms. Her body still trembled and she had an absurd wish that he would turn around and take her in his arms again. Was she crazy? How could she be thinking of his fiery kisses and the strength that melded into her from his strong, capable body? She would just have to get control of herself.

'Where's Annie?' she said, deliberately interrupting her train of thought.

'Doing her homework. She's fine.'

Kelly set the food box down and hurried into Wilson's office. Annie looked up and saw her, then slid off her chair and ran into Kelly's embrace.

'They said you were stuck in the elevator,' she said.

Kelly squeezed the little girl. 'I was, but they came to get us. We're all right now.'

'Was it scary?' Annie looked at Kelly with large, worried eyes.

Kelly smiled. 'A little. But we pressed the emergency button and the loud ring brought the maintenance man.'

Annie tipped her head as if she knew better. 'Ross said he was going to get you. Did he save you?'

Kelly gave an exasperated sigh. 'Well, he helped.'

Annie nodded. 'I thought so.'

Kelly didn't know whether to be pleased or frustrated that Ross had her niece in his corner.

'We've got food out there. Come on out and pick out a sandwich.'

Work stopped for a few minutes as the

team plunged into the boxes of food. Then everyone stood around eating with one eye on the satellite transmissions. Neil sat beside Jean, listening to her account of the elevator fright. Kelly narrowed her gaze. His face was filled with concern, and he had a hand on her knee, squeezing it. If he had a guilty part in any of this, he was certainly a good actor.

After supper, Kelly busied herself helping Jean drag out cots and blankets to set up a place where everyone would bunk down for naps since it looked like they'd be working all night. Even though she made sure she didn't go anywhere else alone, she found herself glancing repeatedly over her shoulder, gauging everyone's expression.

They tracked the storm as it moved across Cuba. Even without a direct approach to the Gulf Coast of Florida, the general rise in the level of the ocean was already threatening Florida's shores as the storm moved northward. New data every half hour reporting winds, pressure areas, and temperatures was helping them forecast whether the storm would actually hit there. And Kelly could see from the tension in Wilson's face that they'd better be correct this time.

For a while, she kept to simple tasks like watching for reports to print out, ripping them off, and handing them to the others for analysis. But a spur of resentment finally goaded her into more useful action. She was a good weather scientist, and no one was going to keep her from doing her job. She began to offer her analyses of the satellite images, doing mathematical calculations to help predict how fast and how far the storm was moving.

At nine o'clock, Annie's eyes were drooping, and Kelly bedded her down with blankets on the couch in Wilson's office, where she could check on her. With the hubbub continuing all night in the next room, the girl would be safe.

Kelly rubbed her eyes and decided to get a cup of coffee. She headed for the women's locker room to get some quarters from her pursc. She was doing the combination on the lock at her locker, when she heard her name.

'Kelly.'

The sound made her heart jump into her throat.

But it was only Ross, standing at the other end of the row of lockers.

'Oh, you scared me,' she said, hand on her chest.

One arm was braced on a locker, and his dark eyebrow lifted.

'Why, did something happen to make you nervous?'

She straightened and tossed her head. 'Well, being cooped up in that elevator was a bit claustrophobic.'

He moved toward her slowly, causing her nerve endings to tingle. She got out her purse, shut the locker door, and leaned against it, willing him not to come any closer.

He seemed to sense her mood and stopped a few feet away, lifting one leg to rest his foot on the bench.

'I just thought we should talk,' he said.

She noticed that he looked tired too. His eyes were bloodshot, and there was a faint line of five-o'clock shadow around his chin. She suddenly tried to envision what he'd look like with a beard and decided he'd look very dark but distinguished that way.

'You always talk in women's locker rooms?' she quipped.

'There's nobody else in here,' he said.

'How would you know? Did you check all the stalls?'

'Kelly,' he said, shaking his head. 'I'm sorry you found out about my job here the way you did. I wanted to explain it at a time and place where you'd understand.'

'Oh, like in my bedroom.'

He met her challenge with his piercing stare. 'That's not fair.' Then the corners of his mouth turned up in a sensual smile. 'But since you mention it . . . '

'Oh.' She let out an exasperated sigh. She'd half a mind to throw her purse at him.

He moved closer then, as if he couldn't keep his hands off her waist. His face hovered close to hers, forcing her to stare into his eyes. And she saw the pools of desire there.

'Kelly, listen to me. I need your help. We need to help each other. I . . . '

Her throat went dry as she waited for what he was about to say next. She could almost see the words forming at the back of his mind. Saw him struggle with how to say it.

He let out a long breath. 'I care about you, Kelly. More than you know.'

'Hmmmm.' It softened her, but not completely.

But what his words didn't do, his fingers did. They were tracing a line from her throat down her collarbone to the soft fold between her breasts. She gave a gasp.

'Ross, don't.'

He groaned and pulled her closer. 'Don't you want me to do that?' he whispered into her ear. 'Don't you want me to give you the pleasure you deserve? This thing between us, I can't control it. It's like we were meant to be together.'

She closed her eyes, her fatigue and the strain from the day making her want to cling to him. How absurd. Here they were in a brightly lit locker room, reeking of the cleaning fluids that had been used to swab the showers down, and her mind was in a romantic fog.

Meant to be together? As if the gods had planned it? In a weird way it made sense. They were linked by the past, thrown together by the present. Was someone trying to tell her something? Maybe their passion was an expression of the shared emotions that had resulted from her father's death. But how could making love with Ross exorcise the guilt and grief she still carried from a single day six years ago?

12

She didn't answer him, but he wasn't really waiting for an answer. Already his lips pressed the sensitive spot against her throat just below her jaw, forcing her head up. How did he know just how to apply the tempting pressure that made her want more? *Not fair*, came some dim protest, a remnant of the anger somewhere deep within her that always pulsed against life's blows.

But Ross wasn't trying to deal her a blow. He was trying to love her. Love? She balked at the surprising thought. But *something* between them was growing, some connection she'd been hard-pressed to deny. Feelings expressing themselves in physical love. Her mind buzzed as his hands found their way under her blouse to warm the skin at her waist. Always in the past the physical side of love had seemed like nothing so much as a substitute for feelings that weren't there. Could it actually be that this time it was the reverse? A needful and soulful connection between them that was so powerful that the expression could be fulfilled only through making love?

Her ideas weren't so much thoughts as intuition, which set her spirit on fire, just as Ross was setting her body on fire. She already felt the hum of desire deep inside her as he pressed her against the lockers. But she didn't feel the metal; all she felt was him.

'Ross,' she said breathlessly. 'Someone might come.'

A guttural grunt was his only response.

His mouth was busy at the base of her throat, and her mind began to let go of logic as she realized some of the buttons of her blouse had come undone. He expertly released the fastening of her bra strap, and she drew in a breath when his hand covered her breast, sensuously, possessively.

Her hands had lost no time either, pulling his shirt out from his trousers, caressing the hard, muscled torso, her arms enfolding him. She wanted to be consumed by him.

His hand left her upper torso to slide along the inside of her leg, just as her hand drifted from his firm buttocks to the front of his trousers to discover the length of hardness making itself felt behind his zipper. He covered her hand with his, moving her closer against him, massaging her hand against him up and down.

'Ahhhh,' he let out a long, sensual moan, his mouth pressed against her shoulder.

'That's what I want.'

She wanted to do everything more, but there was no place to do it. Disheveled as they were, they could still right themselves if someone walked in. Still, Kelly knew that her face must be on fire. Blood pounded through every vein. When his hand slipped between her legs, she moaned herself. Oh, God, how she wanted him.

'Touch me, Kelly,' he whispered.

He must have known they couldn't complete the act of lovemaking there. But he would not be satisfied until her fingers lay against him intimately. Until she claimed him for her own by thrilling him with her touch.

His belt loosened, his trousers came undone. She needed no further encouragement to slip her hand inside and reach for the hard, moist signal of desire that was for her and her alone. She felt him tremble when she caressed him.

'I want you, Kelly. There has to be somewhere, dammit.'

His voice was ragged, frustrated. And if she hadn't feared they'd be caught, she would have ripped his clothes off then and there and consummated their passion.

Some hysterical part of her wondered how they would explain that to the rest of the staff, when inevitably they were found out.

With one last push against her lower abdomen, Ross removed her hand. 'Stop,' he breathed. 'This only makes it worse.'

Still, with her hands safely around his waist, Ross couldn't resist pushing her shirt and bra aside and lowering his mouth to tantalize one breast, his other arm supporting her back.

She shrugged into his caress, feeling the thrill of his mouth on her from her pulsating center outward, curling her shoulders forward.

'Oh, yes, yes,' she whispered.

His head finally came up, and he leaned against her, pulling her shirt down. Then he kissed her, his mouth wide open, his tongue thrusting deeply, entwining with hers. The fierceness of his grip around her torso and the demand of lips and tongue tried to make up for what the rest of his body could not do.

Finally, they leaned their heads on each other's shoulders, breathing hard.

'I love you, Kelly,' he murmured into her ear.

She pulled her head back to look at him, saw the lowered eyelids, the passion-filled eyes.

'I . . . don't know what to say,' she whispered.

Slowly, resignation replaced the desire on

his face. His eyes opened fully.

'That will have to do for now. I understand your feelings, and I'm willing to wait.'

Embarrassment flooded her. 'I mean, I just don't feel prepared.' Still not the right words.

He smiled awkwardly, but with understanding. 'I can see that.'

He embraced her gently, smoothed her hair, stood away to fasten his belt.

All she could do was stare at him. Stare at the beautifully handsome face, the purposefulness and confidence in his jaw, and wonder if she could believe what she'd heard. He loved her? Did he mean it? She shook her head slowly.

He bent to kiss her full, reddened lips. 'You're so beautiful, Kelly. I love seeing you look like that.'

She swallowed, tried to smile, then tried to stand up straight on her own two feet.

'I'd better get out of here,' he muttered.

'Yeah,' she said.

'You make sure your cot is next to mine,' he said, moving forward and tipping her chin upward for one last kiss.

Her eyes opened wider. 'I don't know if that's a good idea.'

His grin answered her. 'We do seem to be having the devil of a time getting any privacy.'

Then he walked away, turning at the end of

the row of lockers. For a moment Kelly stood and stared at the space where he had been, then bent to open the combination lock on her locker. She needed a shower. Badly.

★ ★ ★

The rest of the evening went by in a haze. Kelly worked as part of the team, but with her eyes and fingers on automatic. Inwardly, she felt the parts of her mind and spirit whirling away in a sweet tempest of newfound emotions. Adjusting, purring, throbbing with expectation. It was as if she were two people — the exterior self that did what was expected of her, as watchful and wary as ever. And the inward self that knew something had changed.

Reports continued to come in of rising water levels as the storm surge hit the beaches farther south. She was glad they'd come to the base after all, other than regretting that she hadn't had time to look through her father's papers for some sort of clue to what was going on.

She had located a packet of her father's letters last night and meant to read through them, but between phone calls from Helen, concerned about the weather reports, and making sure Annie was ready for school on

Monday, there hadn't been time. She had also sent for a couple of boxes of her father's things that she had left stored in Boulder.

At eleven-thirty, she asked Ross to carry Annie from Wilson's couch to one of the cots in the make-shift dormitory on the third floor. After tucking Annie in with her stuffed animals, Ross insisted on tucking Kelly in too.

She placed a blanket on the cot and then stretched out fully clothed. Ross bent over her, pulling a second blanket up to her chin. Then he crouched down to kiss her on the lips. A tender kiss. She closed her eyes and let his warmth invade her. The way his cheek grazed hers and then the kiss he pressed against her closed eyes were full of promise, full of hope and redemption from the past.

'Hmmmmm,' she sighed contentedly. Contentment was an emotion she didn't allow herself very often. Was it possible to really feel like this? she wondered foggily.

'Sleep tight,' he whispered.

'Wake me when it's my shift again,' she mumbled, already drifting into the first stages of sleep.

She heard Ross move around to her other side, where he had planned to set up his own cot. Not touching her, but near enough for comfort.

How six-and-a-half hours could pass in a blink, she didn't know. But when Kelly opened her eyes, there was some light coming in the windows. Ross's unshaven face was above hers, and he was shaking her gently.

' 'Morning,' she mumbled.

'Sorry to wake you, my love, but I thought you'd want to know I'm going out.'

Her eyes came full open and she scrambled up on one elbow. 'Where are you going?'

His face held a look of concentration. 'The hurricane is headed this way now, no doubt about it. Emergency crews are short-handed. I volunteered to go out into the field.'

She sat up now, alert, marshaling her senses. 'Right now?'

'Wilson advised the governor's office to evacuate the resort areas along the beach. There's little time. I think I can be more help out there, making sure everyone gets the message.'

She threw off her blanket and swung her feet to the ground.

'What about the police and the harbor patrol? Won't they be able to handle it?'

Ross's expression looked grim. 'We hope so. But the dispatchers say they're short-staffed. A lot of their teams drove farther south to help with the scene there. Now that the hurricane's moving so fast, they're not sure all the rescue workers can get back in time. So they need qualified volunteers.'

'Let me guess,' she said with a deliberate lightness. 'You're qualified.'

'In emergency first aid and some basic rescue techniques, yes.'

She shook her head, muttering more to herself than to him. 'Is there anything you can't do?'

Annie began to stir, so Kelly gave her a good morning kiss and together they headed off to the locker room to freshen up. At the elevators, Kelly looked warily at the door to the stairwell. She tightened her grip on Annie's hand as they stepped into the elevator, hoping nothing out of the ordinary would happen this trip.

It didn't, and they washed up in the locker room, using the supplies in the toiletry kit Kelly kept there for use after the long flights.

When they returned to the weather prediction room, everyone was hovering over photos and charts. Ross was just coming out of Wilson's office, now wearing heavy-duty rain gear. She walked toward him, her heart clenching at the thought of him out there in the gale.

'Got it,' she heard Wilson say into his telephone. 'Hangar twelve. I'm sending one of my own team down. He can drive the vehicle.'

Kelly glanced at Wilson, who put the phone down, then at Ross. A sudden tightness in her chest accompanied a throbbing in her head. There was something all too familiar about this business of heading out into danger. Something twisted inside her. She couldn't say don't go. But she could go with him.

She stepped into Wilson's office.

'Wilson, will you take care of Annie? I want to go with Ross.'

Wilson studied her and then looked down at the little girl, still holding Kelly's hand.

'What makes you think you need to go?' he asked Kelly quietly.

'I could be of some help out there,' she said. 'If it's an all-hands, then let me help.'

He seemed to weigh her request for a long moment. She knew what he was thinking. That she was a target of some sort of malice as long as she was here. But out there, it would be just Kelly against nature. Nothing to battle except the shadows that clung to her from the past.

He nodded. 'You can go if you're sure you want to.'

Having overheard, Ross stepped into the office. 'Kelly, it's not safe out there.' His jaw squared stubbornly.

But she met his dark, glimmering eyes. 'It's not necessarily safe anywhere.'

She bent down to talk to Annie at eye level. 'I'm going to help Ross get all the people off the beach. You'll be safe here with Wilson, all right?'

Annie shrugged and nodded. 'Okay, I'll stay here.'

She hugged the little girl. 'That's my girl. Now you tell Wilson if you're going to go anywhere with anyone else, okay?'

Again Annie nodded, but her eyes rounded. 'Will you be safe too?'

'I'll be fine.'

'She sure will,' Ross added. 'She'll be with me.' And then he winked at Annie.

Something stirred within Kelly. She knew Ross just wanted to reassure Annie that he would be Kelly's protector. But she realized that in her heart she was coming to believe that was true.

She stood up and turned to Ross. 'Give me a rain slicker.'

In minutes she was in warmer clothing and covered in protective rain gear. An attached hood would cover her head with a drawstring to pull it tight at her chin.

As they hurried across the tarmac to hangar twelve, mental pictures of her father driving off across the plains toward twisting, whirling storms of another kind flashed into her mind. But she felt Ross's firm hand in hers, and realized that was why she was going. She couldn't bear to have Ross go into danger without her. This time she would be there.

The Air Force emergency rescue van that had been loaned to the cause was equipped with all manner of first-aid supplies, shovels, torches, and stretchers. An emergency blue light on the top would be activated when they needed to get through traffic.

Already the Courtney Campbell Causeway was lined with traffic leaving Clearwater, which lay on the opposite side of Old Tampa Bay. They stopped to check with the state patrol, which was orchestrating the evacuation. Ross showed the officer his and Kelly's ID.

'We've got word going out to all the beachfront owners,' said the patrolman leaning in their window. 'But it's hard to know if all the tourists have gotten the word. You know, the stragglers, fisherman who don't come in no matter what the weather until it's too late. The Red Cross is setting up a shelter at the Martin Luther King Center. Just make sure you get yourselves off the beach in a couple of hours. That's when we hear it's supposed to hit.'

'Don't worry,' said Ross. 'We'll do our best to help you round up anyone out there who doesn't have a radio or television.'

He gave a quick glance in Kelly's direction, then spoke to the patrol officer again. 'We won't take any unnecessary chances.'

The officer stepped back and motioned them through.

It took another forty-five minutes of slow driving to cross the peninsula, passing through the small city of Clearwater. Visibility was a challenge, even with their windshield wipers slashing at the hard-driving rain that pounded them. At the Memorial Causeway drawbridge, they were stopped again.

'We can use all the help we can get,' the officer there told them. 'If you can get to Sand Key, make sure all the boaters have come in. From there south, folks are evacuating across Belleair Causeway. You'll have an easier time getting back that way.'

Kelly studied the map to see where he pointed.

'Right,' said Ross. 'We should have no problem.'

With the CB radio in the van, they would be able to stay in contact with the dispatchers.

Already the turbulent sky, the driving rain, and the water under the drawbridge seemed to blend into one mass of gray, with white waves hurling themselves along. Kelly realized she was holding her breath as they cleared the barrier and drove up the drawbridge. Traffic was thick going the other way, but Ross drove slowly, lights on, into the pelting rain.

Out the window to Kelly's right, she could barely see the tall apartment buildings and small shopping center of Island Estates. Palm trees bent their leafy tops along the causeway ahead of them. Judging from the conditions, Kelly had the awful feeling that the edge of the hurricane was already there. The storm surge might have already covered the road along the beach at sea level. But she bit her lip and kept silent.

Ross concentrated on driving, and when they reached Clearwater Beach and turned left along Gulfview Boulevard, she could see that the water had reached the road in some places. She gripped the arm of her door and peered along the shore, looking for people who might have been foolish enough to remain.

They saw no one for a while. Then they turned into the residential areas with fingers sticking out into the intracoastal waterway.

'There,' she said, pointing.

A house with lights on inside seemed to have some activity. Ross pulled up in the driveway and Kelly shoved her door open to get out. Running up to the front door, she pounded on it until a man peered out at her.

'You need to evacuate,' Kelly shouted at him through the screen door. 'There's a hurricane coming. It'll hit soon.'

The man nodded anxiously. 'I heard the reports. I just came to get my mother. We're leaving now. That's my car out there.'

He pointed to a four-wheel-drive vehicle at the curb.

'Do you need any help?' Kelly asked, trying to see around him.

'No thanks. She's ready now.'

A thin, elderly woman appeared in a raincoat, and the man pushed open the screen door. Kelly stepped back, satisfied that they were all right. She ran back to the van.

Ross backed out of the driveway and they continued on to the end of the street. They saw no one else and returned the way they had come. The man had his mother loaded up and started his car. As they drove away slowly ahead of the van, it looked as if they'd make it.

They saw two more people on their trek to Sand Key and made sure they headed back toward the causeway. The hotel at Sand Key was deserted.

'A good thing,' said Ross, eyeing its position alone on a small strip of beach.

Now the rain was coming down so hard it was difficult to see to the side of the road.

The water washed across the road in front of them. Kelly began to wonder if they'd get as far as Belleair Shore. But it would be worse now to turn back and go along that unprotected strip of beach behind them.

Her heart felt stuck in her throat, the adrenaline making her sharply alert to all the dangers. If there were any more people out here, she didn't think they'd be able to see them. But she knew Ross wouldn't rest until he was certain everyone had been warned.

'Do you think we'll make it?' she asked as Ross gunned the car across a finger of water that pushed across the road in front of them.

'Don't know,' he responded. 'The causeway should just be another mile.'

It wasn't reassuring. She remembered that she'd had the choice of staying at the base, but there was no doubt in her mind that she belonged here, with Ross. A finger of dread warned her that if anything happened to her, Annie would be left alone. But she wouldn't think about that. Nothing would happen to them. She and Ross both had survival skills. They would make it.

The van battled water and wind, but they had come to a residential area again. Houses on the east side of the road sat behind cement retaining walls. But if a storm surge came ashore here, the water would overpower the retaining walls. Kelly tried not to envision the houses crumbling and floating away in pieces like match sticks.

No sooner had she thought it than she was able to look out her window at a clear strip of beach. But what she saw beyond made her throat constrict in terror. About a hundred yards out to sea a giant wave rose to stand on end, the white tip taller than the high rises they'd passed on Clearwater Beach. A storm surge. It moved ominously forward. Instead of crashing into the water and rolling ashore, the storm surge seemed to march forward, erect. They had only seconds to try to outrun it and there was no place to go. Once it hit land, it would swallow everything within sight, swamping the peninsula.

'Ross,' she managed to say, clutching his arm.

But he had seen it too. 'Get the life jackets.'

Water filled the road now, ahead and behind. They needed higher ground and fast, but this stretch of land was almost entirely flat. A few blocks farther, Ross turned up a side street that did rise to an apartment complex. She scrambled to the back for the life jackets, every nerve taut. She fastened her life jacket around her, then glued her eyes to the back window to see if she could track the storm surge.

Ross gunned the motor up the hill. A little

farther on, they spied a solid-looking home builders' store with a warehouse behind and pulled around to the side, where there was some minimum shelter from the whipping wind. Ross reported in on the CB.

'Our position is somewhere on Belleair Beach,' he told the dispatcher. 'Just off Gulf Boulevard. There's a bad storm surge coming in. We're at a warehouse several blocks from the causeway. Water's too high to drive any farther.'

'Roger,' said the dispatcher. 'See if you can find shelter. Water's rising on the Belleair Causeway. If you're on high ground, you'd better stay put. Get in as solid a structure as you can.'

Ross paused and looked at the conditions outside. His dark gaze met Kelly's just before he pressed the button on the transmitter again.

'Looks to me like the storm's outer fringe is already here,' he told the dispatcher. 'We're taking cover.'

He replaced the transmitter, then stared at the building in front of them. Around them as far as they could see were only bungalows and an apartment building a little way off. The warehouse was broad and flat and built of concrete. They had one hope and she knew what it was before he said it 'We're going to have to find a way to get in there.'

13

Kelly's heart thrummed. This seemed the safest place. In the back of her mind she was poignantly aware that if the storm came inland, at least they'd be together.

She pushed those thoughts aside and opened her door. Then they bolted for the overhang in front of a side door, which was locked.

Ross dashed along the side of the building, peering around the corner. Then he came back.

'The loading dock's back there. Maybe there's a way in. You ready to run for it?'

She nodded. He pulled a crowbar out of the van; then they dashed along the pavement. They had to slow down to turn the corner to avoid sliding. Then another short sprint and they climbed up to the loading dock. Higher still than the parking lot. One more blessing. Kelly couldn't see the beach anymore, but a pulse of dread seized her as she saw fingers of water rising along the street below. The wave had broken ashore. How far it would come, they wouldn't know.

The oversized door was padlocked, but

Ross worked the lock with the crowbar and eventually broke it open. They stepped into the shadowy warehouse, and Ross pulled the big rattling door down once more. Then he drew a bolt across that would keep it shut.

They blinked in the darkness. She could almost hear his thoughts echoing hers. If the building held, they would be all right. But if the water rose too high, they were still in danger. Then there would be only the roof to try to reach.

'Careful,' he said, as they moved forward. 'We don't want to hurt ourselves on anything.'

She was aware of the scent of wood. 'Smells like a lumber yard back here.'

In the briefest moment when gray light had penetrated before Ross had shut the loading dock door, she'd seen protruding beams stacked on what looked like floor-to-ceiling racks.

He took her hand. 'Stay next to me.'

They felt their way across a smooth floor. Then as her eyes adjusted to the dim interior, she began to make out shapes. They came to a large piece of equipment with oversized tires.

'A forklift,' said Ross. 'Let's go around it this way.'

They continued to feel their way along and

came to the end of the lumber section. She strained her ears to listen to sounds outside that might tell them if the water had gotten this far. Kelly felt a small draft, and then they came to double glass interior doors. These inner doors weren't locked.

'Here we go,' said Ross.

He swung a door open and Kelly could see that they were inside a room stocked with home builders' supplies.

Some gray light filtered in, no doubt from doors located closer to the front of the building. They moved along a row of rolled carpeting and came to a central aisle that cut across perpendicularly.

In spite of her fear for their own safety, the situation struck her as rather funny. All around them, homes were being threatened by Hurricane Joseph, and here they were taking refuge amid piles of home-building supplies. Her eyes flew upward and around her, wondering just how sturdy this place was.

'Come on,' Ross said into her ear. 'Let's look for a spot to dry off and make ourselves comfortable.'

They took off their dripping raincoats and hung them over the end of a rack.

'What about lights?' she asked.

He shook his head. 'Utility wires will be

down in this gale. It's safer to leave them off unless we find something battery generated.'

'There ought to be battery-operated lights in here somewhere. What about hurricane lamps?'

'Good thought.'

It was still too dim to read the signs indicating what was shelved where until they got up close, but they moved along the aisles until they located a shelf of supplies they needed. Hurricane lamps and oil.

'What about matches?' she mused.

'In my waterproof pack,' said Ross, picking up a second hurricane lamp.

'Always prepared,' she quipped, trying to lighten the tension they both felt.

'I try to be.'

They moved to the center of the building, and then Kelly, stopped, amazed at what she saw.

'Bathtubs,' she said, shaking her head.

Right in front of them sat model bathrooms, complete with tubs, whirlpools, commodes, sinks, and shower stalls in several configurations. She walked around the models for a few moments, feeling a little like Dorothy having landed in Oz.

'I wonder if they have kitchens too,' she said in a futile attempt to joke.

'Just a little further ahead of these,' came

Ross's reply, as they moved toward the front of the store.

The wind still raged and buffeted against the building, and Kelly looked with concern toward the glass front of the store.

'Will it hold?' she asked.

Ross squinted toward the glass and seemed to consider the state of the storm outside with some internal antenna.

'Hard to say. We'd better board it up or tape it just in case.'

She knew what he wasn't saying. In case the water level rose further, pushing inward to break the glass. Not a pretty thought.

Action was the best way to keep anxiety at bay. Locating all the materials they needed from the shelves of the store itself, they set about moving sheets of plywood to the front.

The plywood didn't quite reach the ceiling, but it was the best they could do. They secured it with clamps and ropes. But it left the interior even darker than before.

'Nothing to do now but wait,' said Ross.

He took her hand and led her to the area of the store with the model bathrooms and its thick, soft rugs.

Ross looked around. 'We'll stay here.'

Her eyes flew to his, just visible in the dimness. 'Here?'

He began to unzip the jacket he'd worn

under his raincoat and peeled it off. 'Why not? We've got everything we need. With luck, the storm has moved on and we just have to wait for the water to recede.'

Kelly shivered. They had lucked into an inviting place of refuge, but she was no fool. The storm still raged outside, and without any visual clues, they only had the rain and wind howling over their heads to tell them what was going on. The CB radio was fixed to the van, so they didn't even have a way of communicating with the outside world. They were alone and isolated, and they had only each other for comfort.

Ross pulled a thick, fluffy towel off a rod affixed to the wall partition in the model where they stood.

'Care to dry off?'

She took the towel, anticipating how good it would feel against her clammy skin. She joined Ross in peeling out of her clothes down to her underwear. She was about to chafe her skin with the towel, when Ross, a thick bath towel wrapped around his waist, took her towel from her. He draped it around her shoulders and then enfolded her in his arms, her back pressed against his bare chest.

'Aren't you cold?' she asked, drinking in the comfort of the soft, sturdy terry cloth.

'I don't intend to be for long.'

She turned in his arms, her eyes closed as he held the towel draped around her still. Her arms encircled his back and her loins came in contact with his with only his towel between them. As her blood heated, she didn't think they'd need very much terry cloth to keep them warm after all.

'Ross,' she whispered in a husky voice.

He kissed her feverishly, his body searing into hers. 'I know,' he whispered when his mouth left hers to tantalize her ear.

Hands, arms, towels entangled as they reached for each other in a frenzy of need.

He lowered her to the thick rug, a pile of soft towels for a pillow. Then she felt all of him naked against her. Naked at last, the way she'd dreamed of seeing him, but had been too afraid to. She wanted him to be hers and hers alone.

'Ross,' she breathed again as her throat arched against his mouth. 'Make love to me.'

But he'd already begun his ministrations to her body. Every touch, every kiss was done to perfection. His male hardness against her, his legs entangled with hers. Her mouth pressing against his strong jaw, nipping at his earlobes. Their frenzy mounted until he could wait no longer. She opened wide for him, and when he entered her, she knew that heaven existed on earth.

They didn't have any protection, but she didn't worry about that. She knew Ross was healthy, and if a pregnancy resulted from this act of love, she knew deep down that she would want that too.

Their moans left nothing held back. Her mind dizzied at the sensual experience. She was hardly aware of how her fingers dug into his back as he took them both on a ride to ecstasy as shooting stars exploded from within. Even when they started to come down, still she panted, melded her mouth against his, urgently, clinging, wanting more. Wanting it again.

After long minutes the ecstasy dwindled to tingling reminders that still sent little shocks of love coursing through her, ending at her tender breasts, which he kissed and fondled lovingly. Finally, she cradled his head against her breasts as he clasped her against him, his arm covering her waist, their legs stretched side by side.

Oh God, we've finally done it, she thought. And there were no regrets. Whatever happened, they had finally expressed their deepest emotions. And she would remember it for the rest of her life.

Ross raised himself on his elbow and peered at her with his warm, glimmering eyes.

'I love you, Kelly.'

'I . . . love you, Ross.'

Tears choked her throat. How it could be love in spite of what she felt lay between them, she could not understand. But there was no more denying it. She loved him.

He continued to study her face, her shoulders, her breasts, his hand feathering the rest of her skin.

'I want us to be together,' he said seriously.

'Like this, you mean,' she managed to croak.

'More than like this. For life.'

If she hadn't been on the floor, she would have fallen down. As it was, her head pressed back and she felt that she sank deeper into the rug beneath her.

'Forever?'

'Forever.'

'Why?' she whispered.

He pulled his mouth back in an exasperated grin. 'Because I love you. There doesn't have to be any more reason than that.'

'I . . . ' She didn't know what to say. But she didn't have to because his face lowered and she closed her eyes as he kissed her again.

This time he made love to her slowly, taking his time caressing and exploring in a sensual, indulgent way until they both built to an undeniable craving. After they had experienced the pinnacle once again, they quieted their passion lovingly, her head upon his shoulder. Ross moved to drape the big, comforting towels around them, and then they held each other, talking softly.

Finally, they replaced the dry layer of their clothing. Kelly leaned against a partition wall, drawing her knees up to her chest. Ross sat beside her, one long leg stretched out before him, the other leg drawn up so he could rest his arm on his knee. It felt cozy to be together in their little setup. The model rooms made it feel almost as if they were in their own fantasy home.

He held her hand in his own, and they were silent for some time, listening to the storm rage around them. She didn't want to think about the future yet, what it might hold for them. If there was a future. Part of her thoughts were still too tied to the past.

'Eerie, isn't it?' Ross finally said.

'Yes,' she answered softly. 'I guess I'll never be used to this.'

She gazed into his eyes, wondering if he would understand her confused feelings. But it was as if they could communicate without words. He knew she was thinking about her father, that every storm would remind her of him.

He sighed. 'You don't know how many times I've relived the day after your father died, wondering if I could have done anything different. I can't even remember it clearly anymore.'

'I know what you mean.' She leaned her head back against the wall. 'Memory begins to change. You'd like to change what really happened so badly you can taste it. And at the same time you can't quite remember all the little pieces of it.'

She shook her head. 'Sometimes I feel like we remember the worst, not the best. It shouldn't be that way.'

His pressure on her hand tightened. 'No, it shouldn't. But it does seem like that.'

A powerful surge of emotion burned in her chest and welled up into her throat.

'I'm sorry, Ross. I wanted to blame someone. I wanted Dad's death to be someone's fault. I guess I was really angry at him for leaving us.'

A sob overcame her, but she continued. 'I didn't want to admit I was angry at him. He should have been more careful. We needed him, Annie and I. Why was he so reckless when he knew people depended on him?'

He encircled her shoulders and pulled her closer. 'I know, I know,' he said, soothing her. 'It's okay to be angry. We both regret what happened. But he's gone on to some new adventure. Maybe it's time we accepted what he did and forgave him for taking that risk.'

She nodded, feeling tears sting, but they were tears of relief. She couldn't blame Ross anymore. And in her heart she knew she'd started to forgive her father, too.

★ ★ ★

Four hours later, the storm had lessened enough so that Ross decided they could make it to the jeep and check in on the CB radio. The rescue crews had been busy, and they were glad to hear that Ross and Kelly were all right. Kelly spoke to Wilson at headquarters, who assured her that Annie was doing just fine. No need for anyone to know they'd been in danger.

When it appeared that the water had receded enough to get back to the road, they headed out.

'Traffic inland is still a snarl,' came the voice of the dispatcher. 'But the bridges are okay. The storm caught some folks on Belleair Beach unawares, so last-minute evacuations were a flurry. Now the people who stayed are driving across anyway, panicked that the lull is only the eye of the storm.'

'Roger. We'll take the Belleair Causeway.'

Ross replaced the transmitter and turned the van around. Kelly peered through the light rain to make sure they didn't miss anyone else who might need their help. The water still washed across Gulf Boulevard, but it was shallow enough for them to drive through.

On their way back, they did stop to help quite a few people. A driver whose engine had died got a lift in the van. They rescued a child and a cat, stranded on the roof of a garage. Once inland they stopped to help an elderly lady who had wandered away from a retirement home. Mostly they stopped to talk to frightened people, using the CB to radio the dispatcher who could tell them where the Red Cross workers were and how long it would be before power was restored.

The rest of the day was exhausting but worthwhile. When they dragged themselves back into the Hurricane Center just before supper time that evening, Kelly thought she would collapse on the cot and sleep for hours. But the sight of Annie, safe, if a little bored by now, recharged her batteries. As soon as she had divested herself of her wet rain gear and jacket, she squeezed Annie in a hug.

'I'm glad to see you,' she cried.

'Wilson said you were out doing rescue work. Did you rescue anyone?' asked Annie.

Kelly smiled, pushing her own damp hair out of her face. 'Yes, we did. Even a cat.'

Annie's hazel eyes rounded. 'A cat?'

'Yes, she's all right now. We got the cat and her little boy back home.'

Kelly stripped down to the buff in the locker room and took a warm shower. Nothing had ever felt so good. Maybe it was the warm glow that still filled her from the passion she'd shared with Ross. She closed her eyes and let the water run over her head, feeling a deep sense of satisfaction. Today with Ross, she'd felt confident. Exhilarated, yes, challenged by nature's elements, yes. But it surprised her to realize that she'd felt in control.

Was that how Sherman had felt? Unafraid to face nature's turmoil because he was doing what he had chosen to do?

She toweled off and stepped into dry, clean clothes. She felt she'd experienced some sort of epiphany. Odd how no one else could tell a person what really mattered. You had to find that out for yourself. Wait for the realizations that came in moments of wonder.

Her contemplation was short-lived, however. Back in their work area, she quickly became aware that all was not well. Jean told her that Wilson had been edgy all day. A number of things were not right. Some of their predictions had been wrong again, and he was at his wit's end.

'It will be the end of funding if this keeps up,' said Enrico to Kelly and Ross. 'I'm worried about our boss. Small mistakes, yes, but he will lose his job if they are not corrected.'

Kelly gave him a worried look. 'That bad?'

Enrico nodded at both of them. 'It looks like it. We must think of something to do.' He shrugged helplessly. 'I do not see why someone who works here would want to make the Hurricane Center look so bad. His career, his reputation will suffer like ours. It seems self-defeating to me.'

Kelly didn't say any more, but filed the thought away. When Wilson finally sent them home, she went to collect Annie. Truly, Wilson looked more haggard and tired than usual. She didn't know what to say and so said very little.

As Ross went with them out to her car, she felt despondent.

'I'm going to stay here for a while,' he told her. 'But I'll stop by to check on you later.'

'You don't have to,' Kelly said with a tired smile. 'Really. We'll be okay.' She was so tired, she thought she could sleep standing up.

He looked at her drooping eyelids and seemed to get the picture. 'Do you want me to drive you home?'

'No, I'll be able to drive. I just don't promise anything after that.'

He let them go, but waited in the parking lot until they drove off.

Only then did Kelly ponder what Enrico had said. That if somebody wanted these things to go wrong on purpose, the perpetrator must not think he or she had a very bright future ahead. For why would someone with a promising career want to make the Hurricane Center look bad?

14

At home, Kelly got Annie something to eat and got her into her pajamas. Then she stretched out on the sofa and fell asleep with the lamp on.

Around midnight she managed to struggle up, turn off the lamp, and drift into her bedroom, where she fell into a deep sleep. But all night images of the strange events dogging her found their way into her dreams. She wasn't tired when she awoke at dawn, however. In fact, the night's mulling over must have been productive. She came wide awake, feeling rested. Feeling like she could go on.

During the next few days, Kelly got used to the idea that she and Ross were lovers. They maintained a professional demeanor at work, but he saw her home each evening. After a quiet dinner, which Mrs. Watson had prepared, Ross spent time with Kelly and Annie, and then waited while Kelly saw Annie off to dreamland.

Then he and Kelly embraced in the darkness of her bedroom, the moonlight out her windows shining on the water of Old

Tampa Bay. They made love as if it were brand new, exploring new realms of passion and enjoyment. Then Kelly curled up against him and relaxed into slumber.

Sometimes she awoke, frightened by an ominous dream. A sign that the threats hounding her had not completely gone away. Maybe her pursuer was being more careful now that Ross was her protector. Or maybe he was waiting for something.

★ ★ ★

Keeping ever alert for any clues at the Hurricane Center, Kelly was prepared for whatever bad news Wilson might have for her when he called her into his office. Michael Palio was there, and Wilson shut the door. The systems manager was a serious young man, whom she didn't know very well. He had thin, light brown hair and a round face, and he wore the proverbial pencil behind his ear. He waited for Wilson's cue as they all sat down.

Wilson swiveled in the chair behind his desk.

'Michael has found something, but I wanted to keep it quiet. Just between the three of us in this room.'

Kelly lifted her brows. She wouldn't insult

Wilson by asking him if he'd taken precautions to make sure the room wasn't bugged by some electronic recording device. But of course, Ross would have taken care of that in his official investigating capacity.

'What is it?' she asked.

'Explain, Michael,' said Wilson.

The systems manager scooted forward on his chair, his thin brows drawing intently together. 'A password.'

'Oh?'

He nodded. 'Whoever created that fatal error message on your computer last week had to log in and use a password. I have access to the passwords, but the user can change them at any time. However, I was able to trace the password used to create that file.'

Kelly's pulse quickened. 'What was it?'

'Windman,' said Michael.

Windman. Somehow it fit. She turned to Wilson. 'So whose password is it?'

Wilson's lips came together in a look of displeasure. 'We don't know. Michael says the password no longer exists. Whoever used it erased it immediately afterward so we couldn't trace him.'

'Can you tell whose computer the file was created on?'

'Yours,' said Michael without any hesitation.

Of course. The person wanted it to look like Kelly was a basket case, creating all of this herself.

'I should have known.'

'He or she must have seen you type in your password so they could gain access when you weren't there.'

She shook her head in defeat. 'So there's still no way of knowing who did it.'

'No,' said Michael. 'Not really. That's all I could come up with. Sorry.'

Wilson's chair squeaked forward. 'Thank you, Michael. You've helped. As I told you, keep this confidential please.'

The young man nodded. 'No problem.'

As he left, he cast Kelly a sympathetic glance.

'Windman,' she said softly, considering the choice of password.

Wilson looked at her over the top rim of glasses that had slid down his nose. 'It must be what he calls himself. Does it mean anything to you?'

She shook her head. 'No. But now that I know, I'll keep my eyes open. He may give himself away.'

Wilson gave a short grunt. 'I'm keeping a close watch myself,' he added. 'And so is Ross. He's still on the case.'

She wasn't able to look Wilson in the eye. 'I know.'

She returned to her desk, watchful and wary. Every chance she got, she peered at scraps of paper and discarded envelopes just in case Windman had a tendency to jot his name down on something. But she discovered no other clues.

On Wednesday night, Kelly spent the early evening alone, while Ross went to the gym to work out. The boxes from the storage company in Boulder had arrived. She dug through the papers in the boxes, looking carefully at grant applications and reading the letters that had been tucked among the papers and reports. She finally found what she was looking for. A folder marked *Western Kansas*.

It began with an article about a western Kansas water management agency that had employed cloud seeders in an effort to bring rain to the crops. Nearly everyone agreed that under certain conditions, clouds could be made to release moisture. But weather patterns were complex systems with futures that were only educated guesses. Farmers across the border in Colorado saw the planes hired to seed the clouds as something sinister. They claimed that the cloud seeding had brought hail that ruined hundreds of thousands of dollars' worth of crops. A heated dispute took place. Sherman had applied for a grant to study it.

Awareness prickled along Kelly's spine. So Dad had been interested in weather modification, and he had been planning to do something about it. Was there some attempt at weather modification going on right there under their noses? If so, the perpetrator, whom she now thought of as Windman, must think that Kelly would be on to him. He or she must think that Kelly knew what her dad knew and had studied it.

She read and reread her father's notes. Clearly her dad did believe in cloud seeding to help farmers with their crops. He believed it worked and that, if used correctly, it could boost an economy.

But if used correctly, then why would someone be frightened that she might find out? The answer was that whoever was engaged in this activity was not playing according to the rules. Was not doing it openly, paid by a local agency. Destruction, not help, must be the goal.

The hairs on the back of her neck stood on end as she carefully replaced the papers in the folder and stowed it in the bottom drawer of her desk. Then she spent an hour pacing in the living room, making her decision. It was she alone the perpetrator was trying to scare away or threaten in some manner. She alone who could draw him out. Ross wouldn't like it, but she had to carry out her plan. She needed to confront whoever was dogging her heels. He wouldn't come forth as long as he knew she was being protected by Ross.

No, she needed to plan it so that the perpetrator thought she would be alone. She had to use herself as bait. Not that she was foolish enough to get herself into a situation she couldn't get out of. She would have some sort of backup. She had to stay safe, for Annie's sake. She knew too well the loneliness of being an orphan, and she had been a young adult when her father died. Annie was just a child. Her own parents were dead, and her life was too precious. She couldn't leave Annie alone in life. Everyone else had already left her.

But it was with a strong sense of securing the future for both Annie and herself that she had to confront her pursuer. She had to know who was hiding in the shadows trying to twist scientific knowledge into something evil. The threats had achieved their desired effect in one aspect. They had driven Kelly to a slightly dangerous ploy, but one she thought must succeed.

The first problem was to make sure Annie was taken care of while she carried out her plot. Her opportunity came when Nina

Quindry called to invite Annie to the neighbor child's birthday party. The family next door was still fairly new, and Nina was introducing them to friends. Since Annie had already met the little girl and needed to make friends herself, would she like to come?

'That's nice of you, Nina,' said Kelly after hearing what Nina had in mind. 'What time would you like me to bring her over Sunday afternoon?'

'Three-thirty or so,' replied Nina. 'I don't want to spoil their dinners with cake.'

'Anything I can bring?'

'We're trying to keep it simple.' Nina laughed. 'Not easy with this many kids.'

'I'll hunt for a gift. Did you say Katy is turning five?'

'That's right. But don't do anything too elaborate. The kid has plenty.'

'I know,' replied Kelly. 'But they should remember their birthdays.'

As they hung up, she remembered that Johann Amundsen had a little boy. She wondered if he would be invited. If so, it would give Johann the perfect opportunity to fall in with her plans, if he were the mysterious culprit she was set to catch.

She spent the next night after work shopping for a birthday present and collecting supplies she would need. She hated keeping her plans from Ross, but she wasn't ready to face his objections. She would tell him when he needed to know.

On Friday at work, Kelly mentioned casually that she planned to spend Sunday afternoon there, looking at radar scans.

'I need to practice capturing those images,' she confessed to Enrico, making sure that Johann was within earshot. 'I came up with blank files last time. Guess I just need to go over the procedures one more time when there's nobody around and I can concentrate.'

'Sunday?' asked Enrico, eyebrows lifted in surprise. 'Won't little Annie want to go out in the sun and play? We aren't expecting any storms for the next few days.'

'Oh, it's okay. Nina's got a birthday party thing going for the neighbor kid. I'll drop her early and come here.'

'You are very dedicated,' said Enrico with a serious look.

She let the matter drop, but she brought it up later again while she was in the cafeteria eating lunch with Jean and Neil.

'Annie has a birthday party to go to this Sunday,' she told them brightly. 'I'm so glad she's being included in parties. It will help her make friends.'

'Who's her friend?' asked Jean, munching on a carrot stick.

'The little girl who lives next door to the Quindrys. You remember, she was at their house last Friday night.'

'Oh, yes,' said Jean thoughtfully. 'The little blonde.'

'That's right. I'll be able to drop Annie off and then take the opportunity to catch up on some work here for a couple of hours before I pick her up again.'

'Kelly,' chided Jean. 'You put in enough extra time when there are emergencies. You shouldn't work weekends when there isn't a storm predicted.'

Kelly shrugged. 'Oh, I don't mind. You know, I don't really think of it as work, doing what I enjoy. Anyway, Wilson will appreciate it if I can get these procedures down to capture the satellite scans more efficiently.'

'Hmmmmm,' agreed Jean.

Kelly let everyone on the team know she planned to drop by the office Sunday afternoon alone. Everyone except Ross. So when they left the office Friday night, she felt satisfied that her trap had been set. Windman would be sure to take the bait.

That evening, Kelly, Ross, and Annie went for a walk on the beach. The stiff breeze was refreshing. She and Annie giggled as the cool water raced up the sand to their toes. Ross and Annie tossed a frisbee, and then all three of them sat huddled on a beach towel, watching the last light fade over the fiery western rim.

'Red sky at night,' Ross began the old sailor's wisdom.

'Sailors' delight,' Kelly replied.

She snuggled into the strength of his arms with Annie in her lap. *Just like a family*, she thought. When she turned to look at Ross's profile, a stirring of deep emotion moved her. He was so handsome, with his firm jaw and his dark hair lifting gently in the ocean breeze. His dark eyes seemed to be watching the sky and the beach. But behind them, she could tell he was pondering deep, personal thoughts.

Later, after they'd gone back to her place and tucked Annie in, Ross drew her to him on the sofa and stroked her long hair, letting his fingers run through it. But his mind was clearly elsewhere.

'What are you going to do?' Kelly asked him.

Ross didn't need to ask what she meant. He sat up straighter and dropped his hand from playing with her hair, 'I'm checking out *Hercules* this weekend. The person we're after must be doing something while we're up there. He interferes with our transmissions or prevents accurate data from reading on the instruments. I'm supervising an independent electronics expert who's been testing all the equipment.'

'And?'

'We've found nothing so far, but we're not finished. I'll be working with him again this weekend.'

A little surge of adrenaline shot through Kelly.

'Good,' she said.

That would fit in nicely with her plans. Now was the time to prepare him for the rest.

'I found some interesting articles and a grant proposal in a folder the other day. About weather modification.'

Ross's dreamy eyes opened wider and he came instantly alert. 'Where are they?'

'I'll get them.'

Kelly brewed some soothing tea while Ross went over the papers. When she returned with a tray, she found him rubbing his finger across his chin, scowling. A little shiver raced through her.

'So this is what's making our culprit so paranoid.' He met her gaze. 'It was what I suspected all along. Another reason for going over *Hercules* with a fine-tooth comb.'

Kelly sat down and picked up her tea. After a sip, she said evenly, 'You think someone is trying to modify our weather while we're up in the clouds.'

'It's possible. If he's figured out a way to release the silver iodide into the clouds in the hopes that the clouds' moisture will form more rain.'

Kelly was familiar with the theory. Clouds contained moisture, but much of it never got to the ground. Like pearls, raindrops gathered around microscopic particles. But many clouds didn't have enough particles to start a raindrop. So cloud seeders injected additional particles in the form of silver iodide into the cloud, hoping that moisture would form raindrops around them.

'So you think Windman has found a way to seed while we're in *Hercules*. Would that really make the storm worse than it already is?'

Ross sighed. He didn't react to the name Windman, confirming Kelly's assumption that Wilson kept him informed.

'The problem with weather modification is that after endless studies, the science of cloud seeding cannot be proven. They seed clouds. It rains. Maybe it would have rained anyway. No one can say. The subject has even found its way into politics and emotion.'

'Yeah,' said Kelly, thinking of Windman. 'Obviously a lot of emotion.'

'So, it's not a matter of whether Windman is creating havoc with our weather. It's a matter of whether he *thinks* he can.'

'And has gotten someone else to believe it?' Kelly excitedly picked up his train of thought.

'Maybe. Someone who pays him to do it.'

He set his mug in the side table, then reached for her hand and pulled her against his long frame until they were sprawled across the sofa. He settled her into his arms and rested his chin on her head.

'I want this to be over, my love. Then we'll plan our future.' He gave her a gentle kiss to the temple. 'We should be a family,' he murmured in her ear.

Just what she'd been thinking on the beach. Perhaps it was inevitable after all. 'I want that, too,' she said. 'As soon as . . . '

'Yeah,' Ross said crisply. 'As soon as we nail the bastard who's causing the trouble.'

*   *   *

On Sunday, Kelly dropped Annie at Nina's little party early and then drove to the base. Ross had told her when he'd be working with the ground crew on *Hercules*, so she planned to keep the two-way radios between the crew and the weather center handy. She would be able to radio him if she needed him.

She shivered her way across the windy parking lot and signed in at the security desk.

As the elevator whined upward, every nerve felt jumpy. The second floor was so silent, her footsteps echoed in her heartbeat. She booted up her computer, attuned to every creak of the building, listening for human movement.

She set up a tape recorder with a two-hour tape next to the computer, a piece of black electrical tape over the red light that indicated it was on and the cassette turning. Then she masked its position with some clutter. After cutting the electrical tape, she closed her small Swiss army knife, which concealed a small knife, miniature scissors, a file, and tweezers, and slid it into her jeans pocket. She tested the radio to the ground crew outside, but didn't ask for Ross. However, she kept the headset within easy reach.

Then she waited. The lab was so silent the hum of the computer roared in her ears. Her heart thudded in her chest. She began to question the wisdom of her idea. Supposing something should go wrong? Supposing the culprit was more than just a sick, conniving opportunist? Supposing he came there with a gun?

Just as her nerve was faltering, she heard something. He was so silent, she had to stop breathing to be sure. But she was certain someone was standing behind her on the other side of the room. Before she turned around, she flipped the switch on the radio transmitter, praying that someone was listening in *Hercules*.

She turned slowly to face Max Omari pointing a gun at her. She swallowed and uttered his code name.

'Windman.'

Max's small gray eyes opened wider, pierced her with his stare through the wire-rimmed glasses. It took all the courage she could muster to stand there and pray he wouldn't shoot before she could get him talking. She needed his confession for the tape recorder. He took a step closer, satisfying himself that no one else was in the large, open room.

'It's just us, Max,' she said in a voice that shook. 'Just me.'

He came closer, and the look in his dilated eyes gave her hope that she could get him to talk about himself, to brag about his accomplishments. She stood resolutely in front of the tape recorder, knowing that everything Max said would be taken down.

'I want to know why, Max. Why are you dogging me? Surely I can't stop your plans.'

He waved the gun back and forth, but it wasn't pointing at her exactly. Now was her chance to get him to talk.

'What do you have to gain, Max? Is it

recognition you want? What?'

'Be quiet,' he finally spit out.

He reached behind her and turned off the radio transmitter.

'You talk too much. Like your father. Not brilliant. Nor was he. I was passed over, of course. No one wanted a German immigrant to head a department. No, it's always been so. You can see it in their eyes. They won't say so, but it is there. Well, now they'll be sorry. I will win in the end.'

Kelly felt frightened, but she held her ground. She had to understand what he was doing and how.

'Is it the cloud seeding, Max? Are you controlling the storms? Making them worse? Why?'

His smile was evil, eerie. 'Very clever of the storm chaser's daughter. That's what everyone wants, isn't it? To be able to control the weather? Well, we can seed clouds to make rain, to make the clouds roar with destruction.'

She winced. 'Why would you want to do that?'

'For money, of course. My client respects Max Omari now. My client pays Windman to sow the seeds of destruction.'

A vision of the incredible property damage a storm could cause flashed through her mind. Understanding began to dawn.

'You want property destroyed. Is that because someone who gets a contract to rebuild pays you a commission? Some powerful contractor wants the insurance money that will be paid out to rebuild roads, bridges, buildings. And you get a cut of that. Am I right?' It was sick, and frightening.

'Why I do what I do is my business. You wouldn't understand the need for money, for future security.'

'Max, you are not so different from my father and me, really.' She tried to keep her voice level, reasonable. 'We all want to understand the weather. My father respected your abilities. If he'd lived to become the head of the department, I'm sure he would have promoted you.'

Omari waved the idea away with the muzzle of his gun. 'Nonsense. He thought of nothing but his own advancement. And you are like him. Too clever.'

'My father was just a poorly paid college professor. He wasn't in it for the money. He did his research because he loved it. He risked his life every time he chased a tornado. You're mistaken to think you've been cheated out of so much.'

But she stopped her pleading, realizing he might shoot her if provoked. He waved the gun.

'Sit down in that chair and lift you hands away from your body.'

She did as she was told, her eyes brimming with tears. She'd missed her chance to radio Ross. How she wished she could will him to burst through that door.

'So how do you do it, Max?' Her voice shook, but she pressed on. 'How do you get the silver iodide from *Hercules* into the clouds?'

He grunted. 'That is my little secret. You really don't need to know now.'

From behind her she heard movement and foot-steps. She drew in a breath. Someone here to help her? But when she glanced over her shoulder a large brawny man she had never seen moved out of the shadows and came around the end of the horseshoe work stations. Panic crawled up her throat. Who was he?

'Tie her up,' growled Max. 'It's time to get rid of her for good.'

She opened her mouth to scream, but the thug with his mean, narrow, dark eyes reached out for her. The word *help* died in her throat as she struggled with him. Then his big hand pressed a pungent — smelling cloth across her mouth and nose.

Chloroform, she realized as her head started to go dizzy. She fought and choked, but she was no match for the man's strength. He had ropes around her, pinning her arms to her sides, and he got her feet under his so she couldn't even kick.

Ross! her mind screamed as she began to black out. *Help me!*

15

Ross crossed the tarmac to go inside headquarters and see if Kelly had arrived yet. As he slid his card through the electronic reader, then signed in, his skin prickled.

The halls were empty. But something lurked in the shadows. Something ominous. He didn't stop to look, but hurried his steps. When he saw from the indicator that the elevator was in the basement, he took the stairs, not wanting to wait.

Nina Quindry just happened to mention that Kelly was coming in to the office. By his watch, Kelly shouldn't be there yet. The kids' party at Wilson's should have just been getting started.

Unless she'd dropped Annie early. That didn't make sense, but then, Kelly hadn't even told him that she'd planned to come there, which he found odd. *Dammit, Kelly. What are you up to?*

He swung into the big room and stopped dead. No one was there. Nothing.

He started to breathe again. He knew he was jumpy, but not without reason.

But as he walked around the big map

tables and toward the computer monitors, his skin prickled again. He heard something. What was it? A nearly inaudible sound, like something turning.

He stopped by Kelly's workstation. A glance told him she'd been there. He swept the papers aside and saw the tape recorder. Pressing the rewind button, he stared impatiently at it, all the while looking for other signs, other clues.

Something had happened. Something had gone wrong.

The tape jerked to a halt and he pushed PLAY. The instant he heard Kelly's voice utter the name *Windman*, his blood turned cold. He turned up the volume, heard her speak to Max Omari. Heard him speak to her.

Dammit. What had happened? With more patience than he thought he possessed, he listened all the way through until he heard Max order someone else to tie Kelly up. Without even stopping the tape, his hand was on the phone. Nina picked up at Wilson's house.

'Nina, it's Ross. I need Wilson. It's urgent.'

Hurry up, man, he thought to himself during the long wait until Wilson picked up the phone.

'Ross?'

'I'm at the base. It's Omari. He's got Kelly. Had some thug tie her up. Damn! Where would he take her?'

He heard the tense breathing of the man on the other end of the phone. Then incredulity in his voice.

'How do you know?'

'She had a tape running, recorded everything. Except where they went.' There was a murderous edge to Ross's voice now.

'My surveillance team was watching her. They saw her enter the building. They must have seen her leave. No one's called me.'

'Were they covering all the entrances?'

Wilson's reply sounded less self-assured then before. 'Front and back. You'd better alert security and check my surveillance men. Beige Subaru station wagons with tinted windows on both sides of the buildings. I'll page them on the way there.'

'If you were Omari,' said Ross, 'where would you go?'

Wilson paused. 'Not the bungalow — that would be too obvious. Wait a minute.'

Ross heard the phone clunk onto a table and squeezed the receiver, his sweat trickling onto the earpiece. In thirty seconds, Wilson was back.

'The *Angelina*. She's not in her slip. He must have taken her out on the yacht.'

'Damn,' muttered Ross. 'You'd better notify harbor patrol. You know the specs on the yacht. There isn't time to waste.'

'Done. I'll be there as soon as I can. And, Ross,' added Wilson, 'don't worry about Annie. I'll tell Nina what's happened. The girl will be safe.'

'I'll take your word for that.'

Ross slammed down the phone and sprinted back to the stairs, the door slamming behind him. He was moving too fast to hear the footsteps behind him until it was nearly too late. A hard object struck him at the base of the skull, sending him headfirst toward the stairs. He tried to curl into a roll, one hand grasping for the railing to break his fall. The he felt a painful fist in his stomach, knocking the breath out of him. His blurred vision saw only a large hulking figure dressed in a raincoat. Impossible to identify. Then he slumped into the darkness.

★ ★ ★

Kelly awakened slowly, fuzzily, aware first of little things. Of not being able to move her hands and arms. Of feeling nauseated, wishing the floor would stop moving. Then as the sharp pain in her head began to recede, it all came back. She struggled to open her eyes and focus. Where was she?

It was dark wherever she was. She tried to draw deep breaths, shake her head, tried not to panic. Slowly, her senses returned and she was able to extend her perceptions to her surroundings. As her eyes adjusted, she finally saw small round holes emitting pale light. Portholes. That would explain the rocking beneath her. She was on a boat.

Where? New panic shivered through her as she wondered how long she'd been unconscious. Struggling to be calm, she tried to think. Max had a boat. Had they brought her there? She tried to remember the *Angelina* in her mind's eye and penetrate the darkness around her to see if she was in its cabin. From the dim shapes she saw, it looked likely.

She heard footsteps above and held her breath. Then voices seemed to come from her right. She strained to listen. Not distinct words, but from the intonations there were orders being given. Dull dread suffused her. If she remained tied up, they could throw her overboard and she'd drown. She had to get free.

She stifled a small cry of desperation behind the gag and tried to wriggle in her bonds. She leaned as far as she could to one side; the chair she was tied to started to tilt with her. So, it wasn't bolted to the floor.

Realizing quickly what she needed to do, she tried to penetrate the immediate darkness to assess whether there were any obstacles in the way. Her eyes were growing more accustomed to the shadowy cabin now, and it looked like a padded daybed stretched under the porthole to her right. She would try to fall that way.

With a mighty heave, she tilted the chair toward the daybed, letting her shoulder slide against its upholstery. Some of her hair pulled as she slid by, but she didn't cry out. Then she thumped to the hard-wood floor, but with the daybed breaking her fall, it had made relatively little noise.

Still, her heart pounded from the effort of having to maneuver like a seal. And from fright that someone had heard her and would come in a minute. She needed some time.

More clumping on deck above. Then the grinding of the motor and they were moving. *Wait*, she wanted to cry out. *Where are we going?*

The moon was visible through the porthole now, and she tried to think about the sky, where the moon ought to be in the October sky. But that only told her in which direction the boat was headed. Not how far it had gone.

Catching her breath, she wiggled and

scraped her hands against her sides until she felt her pocket. Thank God they hadn't searched her thoroughly or they would have found her little Swiss army knife. If only she could get it out.

She waited again until her heart stopped pounding in her ears. It sounded so loud, surely someone else must hear it. And she couldn't afford for them to hear her try to maneuver the tool out of her pocket and onto the floor. No one came, probably because they were busy moving the yacht to a hiding place. For surely by now someone would be searching for them. Wouldn't they?

Max would have had to sign in at the Hurricane Center. She didn't like the niggling doubt that maybe he'd done something peculiar like found a way in that bypassed the guards. Or had someone else sign out for him the last time he came in and simply spent the night there, hiding. And waiting.

A man bent on changing the weather would have been damn careful about not getting caught abducting her. Or so she would assume. He'd even hired goons, although they might belong to the client he'd alluded to. And where did he learn how to use a gun?

Stop it, she ordered her racing thoughts.

She inched around, praying that the noise of the motor would cover her efforts. She needed to get the pocket tool out onto the floor. How she would get it open with just the fingers of one hand would be the next problem. If only she could live that long.

★ ★ ★

Ross came to with a severe pain throbbing in his head. He used precious minutes sitting up, blinking, and waiting for the blur in his eyes to focus. As soon as he could, he stood up. Nothing was broken, so he limped down the stairs, then got up some speed. Necessity made him suppress the pain as he hurried outside. The clock had turned back one hour last night, and it got dark earlier now. The early darkness would help Kelly's abductors.

He located the nondescript five-year-old Subaru at the side of the front parking lot. Its driver, a thickset, square-jawed man with thick black hair, was muttering curses in a language Ross didn't recognize. He was a large man. And when he kicked his flat tire, the car shook.

'You get a page from Quindry?' asked Ross, staring with a bad feeling at the slashed tire.

The man swore an oath, then dove into his car and got out a cell phone. He pressed in a number, presumably Wilson's. When he got an answer, he swore some more.

'I just went across to one of the hangars to use the john,' he said into the phone, ignoring Ross. 'When I got back, my tires were slashed.' A pause. 'Dunno. Yeah, right.'

He hung up, screwed up his black eyes at Ross, and jerked his thumb in the direction of the building.

'You Ross King?'

Ross nodded.

'Let's go.'

There wasn't a question about where they were going. The other man hired to watch Kelly had been positioned on the other side of the building. Ross couldn't get there fast enough.

They flung themselves around the last corner of the building and halted, breathing hard. No Subaru, no car in sight.

'Damn,' said Ross. 'Where is he?'

'I'll try paging him.'

'You do that,' said Ross. Then he dashed off for his own car.

It was faster to drive to the commander's office on the base. Precious minutes were lost talking his way past the duty staff to the sergeant holding things down on the weekend. But when Ross displayed his identification and explained the urgency of

265

his problem, the sergeant called the chief of security. By the time he got there, Wilson had joined them, looking harried.

'All right,' said the security chief, a six-foot-seven hulk of a man with a face that brooked no nonsense. 'Give the sergeant the description of this Omari fellow. We'll search the base and contact local authorities. Where do you think he might have taken her?'

'I've already notified harbor patrol,' said Wilson. 'His boat, the *Angelina*, was moored at the yacht club on Davis Islands. They have the records with the boat's registration.'

'Good,' said the security man, a deep crease between his eyes. 'Then we've done all we can. If you can think of anything else, let me know immediately.'

Ross left Wilson to go over a few more details with the security staff. He paced in a waiting room. Kelly was in danger. The thought sent shivers of desperation racing through him. He rubbed the back of his neck, not understanding what had gone wrong. Where was Jean? She was supposed to be at the office. Why had Kelly come early?

No matter any of that. Blaming someone wouldn't keep Kelly safe. Only he could do that.

The words rang in his mind, and as soon as Wilson was free, he confronted him. 'If she's in the yacht, then we have to figure out where they would go.'

Wilson gripped Ross's shoulder with his big hand. 'I understand your feelings. I'll do anything to get her back. I just don't know where he'd take her. We can search his bungalow. There might be some clues there.'

Ross weighed that possibility. They were wasting precious minutes, but it seemed the wisest decision. The harbor patrol was scouting the waterways. Seas were calm, thank heaven. Every law enforcement agency within a hundred miles would be looking for her. It might pay to use some logic. Blind searching would get them nowhere.

'Right,' said Ross. 'Let's go.'

★   ★   ★

Once Kelly got the Swiss army knife worked out of her pocket, she struggled to do some good with it. More than once she gave up in frustration. If they walked in on her now, it would be the end anyway. But self-preservation, not only for her own sake but for Annie and for Ross, made her struggle on, even though tears moistened the hair dangling in her eyes.

Ross would know she was missing by now. Perhaps there was a search going on. But since she'd passed out before they'd left the building, she had no idea where they'd brought her or how they'd done it.

She was making better progress now with her tiny blade against the burning ropes. Her skin was rubbed raw, but that didn't matter if she could get loose. Suddenly she felt the bonds loosen. She was halfway through one of the ropes. Faint hope began to race against the urgency of getting loose before the boat docked and they came to get her.

She twisted and sawed, concentrating all her effort on the remaining strands. Then suddenly the yacht thudded against creaking timbers at a pier, just as the last strand was cut. She wriggled a hand. There were more ropes tying her, but with one of them cut, she might be able to pull the rest loose. She doubled her efforts, straining and tearing.

Miraculously, she got one hand out and used it to shove the ropes off the other hand. Then she steadied the toes of her sneakers on the hardwood deck and used her arms to pull herself upright, still sitting on the chair. She wasn't out of this yet.

With fingers free to strain and slash at the knots, and using the little tool as a lever, she got out of her bonds. But now she heard the voices, and new terror rippled through her. There wasn't a moment to waste. Her only advantage was surprise.

Remaining in darkness, she crept forward and peered up the steps to an open hatch. From the voices on deck, it sounded like they were docking. Now would be her only chance, while they were busy tossing lines to the dock and tying up. From the porthole to starboard, she could see shapes that resembled foliage. Open water then must be either to port or astern.

Her pulse throbbing in her ears, she crept farther upward, ready to bolt if she should be discovered. These people meant her harm. Max had said it was time to get rid of her for good. He probably meant to drown her and make sure she sank to the bottom of the sea. She couldn't be hurt any worse by trying to defend herself and escape. Still, she had to fight an urge to cower and hide. But there was no place to hide. It was now or never.

She heard someone step off onto the dock and call up to whoever was on deck.

Now! she commanded herself, then lunged forward out of the hatch and veered left.

No one blocked her path, but as soon as she ducked around the cabin and sprinted alongside the railing, a shout went up. She had no way of knowing exactly how shallow the water was. But she saw more open water at the stern and headed that way. Realizing that any minute they would come around the opposite ends of the cabin and make a rush for her, she clambered over the railing and prepared to dive.

She saw one of the goons coming across the bow. A glint of moonlight caught the metal of the gun in his hand. Headfirst, she sprang into the water. The shot beside her was muffled as she kicked herself deeper and pressed her arms in a strong breast-stroke. Every ounce of effort was focused on getting away. More shots splashed into the water, and although she'd taken a deep breath, she couldn't stay under for long. Her only hope was to get far enough away from the boat so that the darkness would hide her.

When she had to come up, she kicked and gasped. The men on the yacht were yelling and arguing, their voices distant now. Kelly went under again and swam blindly away.

The next time she had to come up for air, she shook her head and looked for land. She was held back by the weight of her clothing, and she wasn't a long-distance swimmer. She would have to make for shore as soon as she could.

She could see from there that the shoreline was dense with foliage. There would be no one here to help her, but if she could make it ashore without them seeing her, she could run and hide. They weren't shooting now; her angle must have confused them. Breathing deeply, she began a crawl stroke, swimming upshore of the yacht, hoping for a landfall that would be far enough away from her pursuers.

Halfway to a pebbly beach overhung with low branches, she heard something splash into the water and then the whine of a small engine. It took her a moment to realize what it was, and then panic set in. The yacht must have been outfitted with a small motorized dinghy. They were coming after her.

16

With the tape of Omari's voice threatening Kelly, the police quickly obtained a search warrant for Max's bungalow. Ross and Wilson met the thin, lanky, middle-aged detective with curly brown hair, who arrived along with his sergeant. The detective wasted no time breaking a window so they could get inside.

On the heels of the police, Jean and Neil drove up. Jean jumped out of the car and ran up the flag-stone walk.

'We got here as soon as we heard,' she said, her face a mass of anxiety. 'What can we do to help?'

'Harbor patrol and helicopters are out there looking,' Ross told her. 'But thanks for coming. I'm not leaving any stone unturned until we find her.'

'Poor Kelly,' whimpered Jean. 'I got hung up. Didn't go to the office when I said I would.'

Neil stepped forward, hugged Jean with one arm. A worried look suffused his face. 'Just tell us what we can do.'

'Thanks,' said Ross, nodding seriously. 'We may need your help.'

The two policemen had broken in the door. The detective turned around to warn Ross.

'You'll have to wait here,' the detective said. 'If this man is doing something illegal, we can't have evidence destroyed.'

But Ross wasn't about to be kept out, even if he was forced merely to observe. He showed his credentials as an investigator for the Bureau of Land Management. The detective frowned, but allowed him inside, followed by Wilson. He warned them again not to touch anything. The two policemen tore through the small bungalow quickly, looking for any clues to Max Omari's illegal activities.

Omari was a fastidious man, Ross thought as he scanned the small rooms in the place. Every room was clean and neat, everything put away. A liquor cabinet was stocked with fine cognac and shiny brandy snifters. There was no evidence of sloppy habits. The place was so organized it sent a chill down Ross's spine. Everything was well thought out, premeditated.

With Ross watching, the policemen pawed through papers in a rolltop desk and finally found something interesting. It was a small key with no markings on it.

'Looks like a safety-deposit box key,' said

the detective. He avoided touching it, but scooted it onto the blotter with a small brown envelope. 'We'll check it out.'

Ross felt impatient, and tried to look for clues in places the policemen hadn't examined. He wasn't exactly sure what he was looking for. Something less obvious. If Max was engaged in something illegal, he was probably receiving money. The police would check out bank accounts later. The key might be keeping something locked up like papers for a false identity.

If Ross was going to find Kelly, and he *would* find her, he needed to use his instincts. He needed to look for some more personal clue. He had to think about who Max Omari was and what parts of his personality he would have left there that would tell them where he might have gone with her.

Max would know that the police would be looking for his yacht. Therefore, he would have motored somewhere quickly where it could be concealed. Sailing would be too slow, and he wouldn't have put into a harbor where the yacht would be easily identified.

'Wilson,' he called over his shoulder. He stared at a framed illustrated map of the coast Max had hung in his study.

Wilson came to stand by him and examine the gilt-framed map. It was a reproduction of an old map, with calligraphy marking islands and waterways. More decorative than useful for navigation. Something any sailor might enjoy having on his wall.

'How fast does the *Angelina* travel?' Ross asked.

'She's got twin one-fifty-horsepower engines, making thirteen knots. She'd still be in this range.' Wilson inscribed an arc on the map with his index finger.

Ross moved closer. He pondered the open waters, not liking what he thought. But the helicopter rescuers would be hovering over those waters now. His eyes scanned the rest of the study and came to rest on a glass display case. Moving over to it, he saw that Omari had mounted plant samples, complete with their scientific names.

'Know where these come from?' he asked Wilson.

The older man bent and squinted. Then he straightened, staring into the distance as if recalling something.

'Caladesi Island,' said Wilson. 'Omari used to collect samples there.'

Ross turned back to the map. The long, fat stretch of island was a state park and nature preserve. No one lived there. The park was closed at night. The perfect place to hide. He turned on his heel.

'Let's go.'

Jean and Neil followed Ross into the emergency vehicle Wilson had commandeered at the base. Ross took the wheel and shrieked through the streets en route to the Courtney Campbell Causeway. He pressed the gas pedal and skirted traffic like an expert, zooming into Clearwater on the other side of the bay. Wilson navigated them on the main thoroughfares into the adjacent town of Dunedin. They screeched to a halt at the dock, where he'd radioed ahead to the rescue dispatcher to have a motor launch waiting for them.

Without stopping, they all climbed into the idling Seahawk. Its 500-horsepower engine roared as Ross and Wilson climbed on board, followed by Neil and Jean. The boat's owner and driver, Drake Howsan, was an experienced diver who hired out his boat for pleasure trips. From the message he'd received from the dispatcher who'd called him fifteen minutes ago, he realized this was no pleasure trip.

Everyone shrugged into life jackets; then Ross stood at the helm as Drake backed the boat into deeper water. Then they wheeled toward the long, dark, uninhabited Caladesi Island, a little distance out.

Ross wouldn't allow himself to believe that

they were too late. That Kelly had been tied and gagged and slipped overboard. She wasn't dead. He would know in his heart if she were. She was a fighter and she was smart. He wouldn't love anyone who had less grit. He knew she could take care of herself, but she would be outnumbered.

But Ross had total faith that they would find her alive and safe. Not to do so would be too tragic a fate, and they didn't deserve that.

He and Kelly deserved a long, fruitful, happy life together. He was certain of it. Taking care of Sherman's granddaughter and having children of their own. A vision rose before his eyes, out of the darkness, and he knew that was what he prayed for now, if he prayed for anything. As his hands gripped the railing where he stood with the spray hitting his face, he knew his destiny with a certainty that filled his heart and mind.

Hang on, he said to her in his mind, certain that she would feel his presence getting nearer. *Hang on just a little longer.*

★   ★   ★

Kelly dragged herself ashore through tangled roots and cypress knees, her chest wracked with pain from the long swim. Trailing vines reached out to cling to her as she plunged into the dense, dark foliage. What natural dangers lay ahead, she didn't want to imagine. If this was an uninhabited island, it was because it was uninhabitable. That or it was set aside as a nature preserve for animals. There might or might not be alligators lurking in the bayous. But there were men with guns out there. So she preferred to take her chances with the natural dangers.

Feeling her way onto solid ground and still breathing hard, she pressed into thick bushes. So thick, she thought she would have to turn back and find an easier way. The foliage would hide her, but her pursuers would have flashlights and she hadn't had time to cover her footprints on the banks.

It was windier now, and her hair caught in the branches, slowing her progress further. As she heard the motor craft drawing nearer, terror and grief beset her struggles. She grabbed the branch that had tangled her hair and gave a mighty yank, pulling it loose. Knowing her light-colored hair would mark her passing, she tried to pull off the strands that now decorated the branch. But she had little time to lose.

Her heart still ached, but the moist, fresh air helped revive her, and she pushed through more bushes, heedless of the scratches to her arms. After a while the bushes thinned, and she finally found herself on what felt like a path. From distant lights off to her right, she was able to orient herself as to direction and headed toward the lights. Where there were lights, there might be people and she could get help.

Behind her she thought she heard voices and realized with agony that she must not have come very far from the shore. The long struggle through the bushes had made it only seem longer. She moved blindly forward, hands outstretched to feel obstacles. When the moon came out from behind a cloud, she could see better. She sped up. She needed to be far enough away so that when the men came out onto the path, she would be hidden. Dense foliage seemed to be abundant. But then what? She couldn't just hide. They would find her eventually. She had to get to the other side of wherever she was and find her way out of there.

★   ★   ★

'There it is,' said Ross. 'Ahead about one hundred yards. Ten degrees to starboard.'

He handed the night vision binoculars to Drake, who took them with one hand. 'I see it.'

He handed the binoculars back to Ross,

who passed them to Neil, standing behind him.

'That's her,' agreed Neil, who had seen the *Angelina* for himself several times. 'Doesn't look like anyone's aboard, though.'

Ross looked again. They were closer now and he focused on the yacht. No one was on deck.

'Pull alongside,' he said to Drake. Then he waved to Wilson and Jean, standing at the railing on the starboard side.

They'd all seen the *Angelina* now, and Drake steered a course to bring them alongside. Ross was first over the railing, followed by Wilson, then Neil, who helped Jean. The motor launch driver stayed with his craft until they told him what they wanted him to do.

They spread out over the yacht, looking for any signs. Neil found the space where the dinghy had been stowed. Ross went below and found the overturned chair, the sawed ropes.

'She was here,' he said, turning and nearly bumping into Jean, who was on his heels.

'She must have got away,' said Jean, taking in the scene.

'Let's hope so,' said Ross, taking the steps two at a time to get back on deck.

They heard the noise from the helicopter

patrolling out to sea. But he knew she wouldn't swim for open waters. She would have had to make for shore.

'Let's check out the shore,' he called to the others. 'You three check out this dock. I'm going to have Howsan take me farther north from here.' He tapped the walkie-talkies they had fixed to their belts. 'Stay in contact.'

Then he was over the railing and back on the Seahawk. 'She's been here, but must have got away,' he told Drake. 'This shoreline might play tricks on us. But I don't think they went very far. The yacht had a dinghy that's not in its moorings. They must have used it to go after her.'

The Seahawk's motor hummed lower as they crawled along, floodlights bathing the thick foliage that grew right to the water's edge.

'I know she's here,' Ross hissed to himself. 'Where did she go ashore?'

Then they saw the dinghy resting on a small pebbly beach.

'How close can you get me?' he asked Drake.

Howsan consulted his depth reading. 'I can get a little closer, but you'll have to wade the rest of the way.'

'Fine.'

Ross waited until Howsan had the Seahawk

as near shore as she could go without being grounded. Then he went over the ladder and let himself into the chilly water. His feet touched bottom and he waded in. He was soaked to the bone, and without the sun to dry him off, the wind simply made everything stick to him. But he hardly noticed.

He studied the ground where the dinghy waited. It wasn't hard to follow the tracks. They led along a bayou with barely enough room to walk. He had to duck and push back branches. One misstep and he would trip over an exposed root and land head-first in murky waters. Then he squatted down and listened. Ahead he heard voices, mutterings, and shouts. Saw the beam of a flashlight. Heard feet running on gravel away from him. He pursued as quietly and quickly as he could.

When he heard a gunshot, he sprang forward. As soon as he came out on the path, he saw Wilson, Neil, and Jean coming along an adjoining path from the right. They must have heard the gunshot too.

'This way,' he whispered, leading them forward in the darkness toward the sounds ahead.

★ ★ ★

A flashlight blinded Kelly as Omari shouted. A gunshot exploded behind her and pinged off the cement path. She kept running, but the footsteps behind her were gaining. After the long swim, she didn't have the stamina to outrun them.

She went down under the weight of a large man, who yanked her arms behind her. She whimpered and tried to cry aloud, but two thugs pulled her to her feet.

'Get up,' growled one of the thugs.

She thought about kicking and trying to run again, but they held on to her with iron grips, pushing her ahead of them to a shack in a clearing.

Omari strode ahead and kicked open the door, and her two guards pushed her into a chair. There weren't any lights, but she could tell who was who now. Omari was near the door with his gun. She could still smell the smoke from the shot he'd fired at her.

The sound of a helicopter got nearer, giving Kelly a surge of hope. There was a rescue party after all. A chance to get out of this if she could avoid Omari's vengeance.

'This is harbor patrol,' came a voice over a loudspeaker. 'Come out with your weapons raised.'

'Get rid of them,' Omari ordered one of the men.

Kelly saw now that one of the hired men had a rifle in his hands. He stepped outside alone.

A moment later, she winced at the explosion of gunfire and the tinkle of searchlights being shot out. The light that had crept in under the door and through the small window was gone.

'Come on,' said Omari.

He grabbed Kelly roughly and made her stand up. Then he pushed her out of the shack along a narrow path through more thick vegetation. They seemed to be heading west now. The helicopter still hovered, but without searchlights, they might not be able to see anyone down there.

Tears stung her eyes as they approached some sand dunes at the tip of the peninsula.

Suddenly figures sprang from behind. She heard a grunt as Omari was knocked over. As she turned, her eyes widened when she saw Ross roll down the sand, struggling with Omari. To her even greater surprise, Neil Devlin attacked the other guard, wrenching the rifle away. She reacted without even thinking and flung herself at the remaining guard, who was trying to aim at Ross. His shot went wild.

She planted a kick in the man's crotch. As he doubled over, she kicked his wrist. He dropped the gun and she dove into the sand after it.

Wilson appeared and took the rifle Neil had freed from the other man. 'Hands up,' he ordered, keeping the two guards under cover.

Kelly pointed her gun at Omari. She dared not shoot for fear of hitting Ross as they rolled toward the edge of the sand dune.

Ross groaned and lay still as Omari lumbered upward. With the gun pointed at Omari's head, Kelly shouted. 'Don't move, Max.'

Ross lifted his leg and kicked Omari backward. The older man slipped down the edge of the dune. Kelly stumbled toward Ross, who took the gun with one hand, grasping her shoulders with the other hand.

'Are you all right?' he said, pulling her against his chest.

She could hear his heart pounding in his chest, matching the beat of her own.

The helicopter had let down two men, who now came up the beach, rifles covering the criminals as they took charge of the scene. As the confusion around them was gradually restrained, all she could do was lean against Ross, thankful that he was alive and unhurt. It took a few moments to realize he was gently examining her body for damage as well.

'Thank God,' Ross murmured as he satisfied himself that she wasn't hurt. 'You're sure you're not hurt?'

'I'm okay. You?'

'Fine. God, I thought I'd lost you.'

Then they kissed and held each other tightly, clinging for dear life as the ocean breeze cooled them. The criminals were led to the beach by the harbor patrol as a police boat motored in to pick them up.

'It's over, Kelly,' Ross said, kissing her temples and pulling his fingers through her long, tangled hair. 'It's over.'

'Is Annie all right?' she asked him.

'Not to worry. She's still at Nina's. As soon as we learned of the danger, Johann and Enrico went there to stand guard.'

She gave a small hysterical sob. 'And to think I suspected them as well.'

'We didn't know who was in on it,' Ross said. 'But now we do. Don't worry anymore.'

They walked back to where their friends waited. Kelly moved forward to embrace each of them.

'Thank God, you're safe,' said Jean, tears and sand all over her face. 'I was so worried.'

Wilson hugged Kelly and patted her back, and she felt nostalgic grief well up in her all over again. When she stood back to look at her old friend, they just gazed at each other, knowing there were no words necessary.

The Seahawk came around to take them back to shore, where they spent the next few hours giving statements to the police and being checked out for their minor injuries at the emergency room. But a few bandages didn't prevent tender kisses and gentle caresses from Ross while they waited to be released.

In the aftermath of her ordeal, Kelly trembled, glad to be sitting down with Ross's strong arm around her shoulders. The horror seemed even worse, now that she was safe and dry. How close a call it had been. She could have died out there.

'The gunman,' she whispered to Ross. 'The one on the boat who shot at me in the water. What if he hadn't missed?'

Ross's grip on her shoulder tightened gently. He kissed her brow. 'I'll spend the rest of my life thanking fate that he did. I couldn't have stood to lose you, my love. I would have gone to the afterlife myself to get you back.'

Maybe that's why she had lived, she thought in a sort of foggy wonder. She had been so determined to live because she had to see Ross again. She couldn't let him go.

★ ★ ★

It was very late by the time they got away. They stopped at Wilson's to pick up Annie, who was asleep. Ross carried her to the car in his arms, and took them home.

A madman had been caught and would be prosecuted. Kelly and Annie weren't in danger anymore. They were all dead tired, but he carried Annie into the apartment and helped Kelly tuck her into bed. Then he pulled Kelly across the hall to her own bed and undressed her, careful of her cuts and bruises. Finally he stripped down and slid between the sheets with her.

'I love you,' he whispered into her ear, satisfied with just watching her lie there. 'It's over, my love. We've banished the demons.'

She turned to him. 'I love you, too. And I have you to thank for helping me banish the demons. All of them.'

'You were so brave,' he said, tracing her face with his finger.

'I realized I had something to live for. I realized it when that storm surge almost got us out on the peninsula. I knew then I didn't want to die. And not just for myself. But because I had someone to love.'

He felt a surge of hope. 'Do you think you're ready for the future now?'

She read his thoughts. 'I've been doing some thinking. I know now that a job well

288

done is the best way to repay my father for what I owe him, to give back what he gave to me. I've stopped blaming him or anyone else for what he did.'

He smiled at her, a loving look in his brown eyes. A look that he hoped conveyed that he wouldn't take no for an answer.

'I want you by my side, whatever we decide to do. I want to marry you and make a home for Annie.'

She choked on tears as she leaned her head against his shoulder. He stretched an arm around her shoulders to pull her close.

'Only fair winds from now on,' he said.

Fair winds, Kelly thought dreamily, her heart full. 'I love you, Ross,' she murmured contentedly.

It was time to let go of what had been. Time to move ahead with her life. And this time she and Annie wouldn't be alone. This time, there would be family surrounding her. Long days of work and play and sharing. Lots of sharing. Yes, love would blow all the storms away.

We do hope that you have enjoyed reading this large print book.

Did you know that all of our titles are available for purchase?

We publish a wide range of high quality large print books including:
Romances, Mysteries, Classics
General Fiction
Non Fiction and Westerns

Special interest titles available in large print are:
The Little Oxford Dictionary
Music Book
Song Book
Hymn Book
Service Book

Also available from us courtesy of Oxford University Press:
Young Readers' Dictionary
(large print edition)
Young Readers' Thesaurus
(large print edition)

For further information or a free brochure, please contact us at:
Ulverscroft Large Print Books Ltd.,
The Green, Bradgate Road, Anstey,
Leicester, LE7 7FU, England.
Tel: (00 44) 0116 236 4325
Fax: (00 44) 0116 234 0205

Other titles published by
The House of Ulverscroft:

JENNY'S STAR

Patricia Werner

Jenny Knight, director of the Cherry Valley Retirement Home, works hard to make her residents happy. But this Christmas it's difficult pretending to be joyful. Still smarting over a failed romance, Jenny just wants Christmas to be over. It gets no easier when Parker McAllister, the son of one of her residents, turns up — toting an enormous tree, and intent on spreading good cheer. Parker finds her ravishing, and despite her resistance, shows her how special the season can be. And, as Jenny's defences melt away, she knows what she wants for Christmas — to win this wonderful man's heart!

IF TRUTH BE KNOWN

Patricia Werner

Susan Franks, research director of the Association for Honesty in Government, was involved in one of its biggest cases. Law-enforcement agencies were suspected of circulating false reports on private citizens. Susan was to present her findings to a congressional subcommittee. After meeting Geoffrey Winston, she wasn't sure if they shared a dynamic attraction — or if he would use his position as a congressman to undermine the AHG: he had warned her not to dig too deeply into the matter. Susan did investigate further. When the case proved to have international ramifications, she desperately hoped Geoffrey wasn't involved . . .

PRAIRIE FIRE

Patricia Werner

In 1887, in the ranchlands of the Oklahoma
territory, the beautiful Kathleen Calhoun
is ready to start a life of her own. A
chance meeting brings the handsome
Raven Sky into her life. Sky is gentle and
educated, but he is also a Creek Indian
. . . Kathleen's attraction to Raven Sky is
undeniable, but her dreams are haunted
by the Indian savages who brutally
murdered her parents. Torn, Kathleen
flees Oklahoma and the arms of her
beloved. Deep within, she knows she must
return to the firm embrace of Raven Sky
to feed the flames of her desire . . .

THE WILL

Patricia Werner

When Leigh Castle returns to the mansion she grew up in, it is not a happy occasion. Her mother has died, leaving an estate entangled by a questionable will. It is more than reason enough to rekindle the old rivalries among Leigh and her three sisters, Hania, Anastasia and Claudia. When Anastasia is discovered dead at the bottom of an abandoned mine, chilling fear takes hold of the sisters, compounded by suspicious events. But Leigh's return has also afforded her the chance to meet Braden Lancaster, the engaging young lawyer hired to handle the estate. Despite the circumstances, the attraction they feel is immediate . . .

A RATIONAL ROMANCE

Melinda Hammond

England, 1803. Elliot Malvern, seventh Marquis of Ullenwood, is very content with his bachelor lifestyle, spending his fortune on the pleasurable pursuits of gambling and mistresses. Rosamond Beaumarsh is determined to remain unmarried and independent. What, then, could persuade them to plunge into an adventure that takes them to post-revolutionary Paris and flings them into a headlong flight across France? Only the exercise of logic. The pair embark upon a romantic adventure and learn that rational thought has very little to do with true love . . .

I MARRIED A PIRATE

Samantha David

When Camilla meets the Pirate surfing the Net she refuses to fall in love with him — but the Pirate doesn't give a yard-arm what she thinks. She's beautiful and he's determined. So he inveigles her into boarding his pirate ship in the Caribbean . . . The Pirate is free-spirited, outrageous and irascible, and in Camilla — brave, resourceful and nutty — he has met his match. Together they inhabit a seductive, bohemian world of musicians and artists, buccaneers and eccentrics.